Ren

A CHRISTMAS NOVEL

ANGEL INSTITUTE
BOOK TWO

ERICA PENROD

ANGEL INSTITUTE PUBLISHING LLC

Dear Reader,

We're so delighted you're here! Welcome to Angel Institute, where romance, Christmas magic, and angels-in-training come together to share the Spirit of Christmas right in the heart of Benton Falls.

This series draws inspiration from some of the most beloved Christmas classics, including—but certainly not limited to—*It's a Wonderful Life*, *A Christmas Carol*, *White Christmas*, and, of course, the greatest story ever told—the birth of our Savior, Jesus Christ, when angels proclaimed tidings of great joy.

As you journey through these stories, we hope you'll feel the wonder of the season, the warmth of love for your family and sweetheart, and, most importantly, the deep love God has for you.

Heaven is always mindful of you, dear friend. There are angels all around you, cheering you on and working for your good. Our prayer is that as you read, you'll recognize their presence, feel their support, and rejoice with them this Christmas.

Merry Christmas!

Lucy & Erica

Prologue

ARTHUR

I take a deep breath, savoring the sweet scent of blooming jasmine mixed with the crisp, heavenly air. The celestial classroom looks the same as ever, but today feels different. The room itself is an ethereal masterpiece, with walls that shimmer like the dawn sky, painted in hues of gold and silver. The ceiling is a vast, open expanse, dotted with twinkling stars that cast a gentle glow over everything. Plush, cloud-like chairs cradle us as we sit at polished wooden desks, their surfaces etched with symbols of wisdom and learning.

I shift in my seat, wondering if I'll ever get used to these robes. My name is Arthur, and while I was often mistaken for Santa Claus during my time on earth, I usually prefer plants to people—and that's what's got me worried about this final assignment.

Henry, our mentor, stands at the front of the classroom. He's got blue eyes, silver hair that's always a bit messy, and he wears robes that shimmer with celestial light. His calm, reassuring voice pairs well with his majestic wings, which are folded gracefully behind him.

"Welcome, my dear trainees," Henry says, looking at each of us in turn. "Today is a big day. Each of you will receive a letter with your final assignment on Earth. You have until midnight on Christmas Eve to fulfill your mission, and then you'll return here to give a dissertation on your experience. Pass, and you'll earn your wings."

I try to swallow the lump in my throat. Leaving the serenity of the heavenly gardens to interact with humans feels like being asked to swap garden shears for social skills—two things I've never been good at. And those wings... I glance at Henry's and silently pray that I can earn my own. I've heard whispers about Enoch's Garden —only accessible with wings — filled with plants I could only dream of, and I long to tend to them.

Henry keeps talking, weaving in stories and metaphors like he always does. He tells us about the importance of learning through experience and making mistakes. His words are filled with old proverbs and classic literature quotes, adding a touch of timeless wisdom to his lessons.

Betty, sitting next to me, leans over and whispers, "I hope mine involves something simple. I'm still getting used to making these robes."

"Knowing you, Betty, it'll be something that requires a lot of heart," I reply, managing a small smile. Her deep brown eyes are filled with warmth despite her worries.

Gabe, the rugged ex-cattle rancher on my other side,

chuckles. "Well, if I get another job that involves fixing halos, I might just start a rebellion."

"Maybe you'll get to ride bulls on Earth," I suggest, my attempt at humor making him laugh.

Henry hands out the letters one by one. When he gets to me, his eyes soften. He places the letter in my hand and squeezes my shoulder.

"Arthur, your time has come," Henry says warmly. "Remember, your strength lies in your patience and kindness. Trust yourself and what you've learned."

I nod, but my stomach churns as I look at the letter in my hand. Patience and kindness were never my strong suit during my time on earth. The parchment feels both fragile and heavy. As Henry moves on to Mary, the nurturing, motherly figure with her golden brown hair and serene demeanor, I take a deep breath and open my letter.

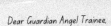

Dear Guardian Angel Trainee,

Your final examination has arrived. This Christmas season, you are tasked with a mission of utmost importance—one that will determine your readiness to receive your wings and ascend to the honored rank of guardian angel.

You are hereby assigned to assist:

Police Officer Ren Michaels

Your objective is to help this individual discover and embrace the true spirit of friendship this Christmas. This task will require all the skills and compassion you have cultivated during your training at the Angel Institute.

Be advised: the stakes are high. A successful mission will earn you your wings and the privilege of becoming a guardian angel. However, failure to complete this task satisfactorily will result in a century-long delay before you may attempt this final test again.

May the light of Heaven guide you in this crucial endeavor. We have the utmost faith in your abilities.

Wishing you divine success,

The Angelic High Council

I chuckle nervously to myself. "A police officer?" I think. "Teaching a cactus to be friendly might be easier." A couple of scenes from my time on earth flash in my mind, a handful of times when the law and I seemed to be on different sides of the fence.

Anxiety gnaws at me. This task feels monumental. This will require me to talk to a human, to care about their interests and concerns, *rrrr*. I worry all the hours spent practicing in the classroom haven't prepared me for what's ahead.

Rebecca, our reluctant resident weather forecaster, receives her assignment with a dramatic sigh. "Hmph." She scrunches her nose. "The spirit of giving. At least I might not have to use the words 'sunny and warm' for a week or two."

Lillian, candy-loving as ever, grins as she reads hers. "Looks like I'll be guiding lost souls. Wonder if I can use lollipops as bribes?"

Gladys, ever the tinkerer, giggles. "This'll be fun! Can't wait to start fixing."

John adjusts his colorful socks, a habit he does when he's nervous. "I've got a journalist," he says, wiggling his toes to show off the vibrant patterns. "Maybe he'll want to do a story about my socks."

Henry wraps up with a final piece of advice. "Remember, you are not alone. I'm always here if you've got questions."

We all nod and rise from our seats, ready to start our missions.

"And don't forget about the Miracle Card and the

Blessings Hotline." Henry adds as we step out of the classroom and into the bustling hallway of the Angel Institute building.

I hold the letter close, feeling the weight of responsibility and an unexpected shock of excitement. Ren is waiting and I've got a chance to earn my wings.

"Okay, Arthur," I mutter to myself, "time to face the music. Let's hope my green thumb works on humans, too."

Pushing through the doors, I sigh as warmth and light wrap around me. I plan to take one more look at my garden before I leave but unexpectedly, I'm overcome with this feeling of urgency, to begin my assignment as quickly as possible, as if there is something I'm needed to do—and it can't wait.

I close my eyes, think of Ren and the possibility of what is coming and suddenly...

One

ARTHUR

My feet sink into fresh snow as I appear in front of the small town library. The frosty December air nips at my cheeks, a far cry from the sweet jasmine-scented breezes of the celestial gardens. I can't help but chuckle, remembering Betty's hope for a simple assignment. "Well, Betty," I think, "at least you're not stuck playing friendship counselor to a cop."

Taking a deep breath, I inhale the scent of pine and wood smoke. It's not quite the heavenly air I'm used to, but it has its own earthly charm. As I steel myself for my first day as a library volunteer—and more importantly, my shot at earning those coveted wings—I see Gabe's face in my mind and think "Bulls might be easier than this, buddy".

I push open the heavy wooden doors, and a wave of warmth hits me like a stroll through a greenhouse. The library smells good—old books, cinnamon, and nutmeg.

Classical music plays softly, reminding me of the ethereal melodies that often drifted through the hallways of Angel Institute.

And there's a woman—Sadie, the librarian, the one I was told to report to. I do not know if this Sadie woman is connected to my assignment or just a means to an end. I need a reason to be here in Benton Falls, and the librarian needs volunteers.

She's perched on a stepladder like some earthly version of an angel, stretching to hang a garland. Her long chestnut hair swings about, her face flushed with exertion. I can sense her emotions radiating out, all determination and joy. It reminds me of Mary's nurturing presence back in our training group. Her foot slips, but she rights herself quickly.

"Whoa there, careful!" I call out, wincing at how gruff I sound. So much for Henry's advice about patience and kindness.

Sadie nearly jumps out of her skin, turning to look at me with big hazel eyes. "Oh!" She exhales as a wide smile parts her lips. "You must be Arthur, our new volunteer," she chirps, climbing down the ladder. "I'm Sadie. Welcome to Evergreen Library."

I nod, trying to dial back the Grumpy Old Man vibe. "Nice to meet you, Sadie. Looks like you could use a hand with those decorations."

Sadie's eyes light up. "Oh, would you? That would be wonderful! Here, why don't you help me with these garlands?"

As we work side by side, Sadie keeps up a steady stream of chatter.

"So, Arthur, what brings you to volunteer at our little library?" she asks, handing me a string of tinsel.

I fumble for a moment, remembering my cover story. "Oh, you know, just looking to give back to the community. Retirement gets boring after a while."

Sadie laughs, a warm, inviting sound. "Well, we're certainly glad to have you. Oh! Did you hear about the gingerbread house contest? Set up begins this Friday."

"Can't say that I have," I reply, carefully draping the tinsel over a bookshelf.

"It's a town tradition," Sadie explains enthusiastically. "Everyone builds these elaborate gingerbread houses. Last year, my friend Ren and I..."

She trails off, a soft smile playing on her lips as though she doesn't want to say too much, but there's a hint of longing in the air. I seize the opportunity.

"Ren? Who's that?"

Sadie's face lights up brighter than a halo. "Oh, Ren is my best friend. He's a police officer here in town. Actually, he usually stops by in the afternoon. You'll get to meet him soon."

Perhaps she's more than a means to an end.

"Tell me about him," I say, trying to sound casual.

"Well, Ren is... he's just the best," Sadie says, her voice softening. "He's kind, reliable, always there when you need him. We've been friends since we were kids."

I'm about to probe further when the library door

swings open, bringing in a gust of cold air and a tall, broad-shouldered man in a police uniform.

"Speak of the devil," Sadie laughs. "Ren! Come meet our new volunteer."

I stand tall, puffing my chest, not sure what to expect as I prepare to meet my assignment.

Ren strolls over, all calm and collected on the outside. But my angelic senses are tingling. Underneath that cool exterior, he's a bundle of nerves.

"Arthur, this is Ren," Sadie introduces us. "Ren, meet Arthur. He's helping us out for the holiday season."

Ren extends his hand, and we shake. "Nice to meet you, Arthur. Welcome to Benton Falls."

"Thanks," I reply, studying him closely, hoping my angel intuition will kick in overdrive. "Sadie was just telling me about the gingerbread house contest. Sounds like quite an event."

Ren chuckles, his eyes darting to Sadie. "Oh yeah, it's a big deal around here. Sadie and I usually team up, but we got our butts kicked last year by old Mrs. Johnson and her Victorian mansion in the amateur division."

Sadie playfully swats Ren's arm. "This year will be different. I've been practicing my royal icing technique."

"I don't know," Ren teases. "Mrs. Johnson's been eyeing that fancy new piping set at the craft store."

Their easy banter continues as we decorate, and I watch them like a hawk. Every laugh, every joke, every casual touch—it's all screaming friendship. But there's this undercurrent, this spark of something more that they're both ignoring harder than I ignored my social skills in favor of gardening back in heaven.

There's definitely something more going on here. What that is, I can't be sure, but I plan to find out.

Suddenly, a horde of children bursts into the library. One little girl stops in front of me, her eyes wide.

"Are you Santa?" she asks, voice full of wonder.

I freeze, caught off guard. "I'm... a friend of Santa's," I finally croak out.

The little girl's face falls, but Sadie swoops in like a Christmas miracle. "Arthur here is helping Santa get ready for Christmas. That's why he looks a bit like him. Would you like to hear a story about some of Santa's special helpers?"

As Sadie leads the children to the reading nook, Ren sidles up next to me. "She's something else, isn't she?" he says softly, watching Sadie with a dopey smile.

I nod, feeling his emotions wash over me. "You two seem very close," I venture.

Ren's smile turns wistful. "We've been best friends for as long as I can remember. I don't know what I'd do without her."

There's more wanting in his voice than in a garden during a drought. I decide to push a little. "Sometimes," I say, channeling Henry's wisdom, "the deepest friendships can grow into something more."

Ren looks at me sharply, hope flashing in his eyes before it's quickly extinguished. "Sadie and I... we're just friends. That's all we'll ever be."

Before I can respond, Sadie rejoins us, her cheeks

flushed from storytelling. "What are you two whispering about over here?" she asks playfully.

"Just guy stuff," Ren says quickly, his ears turning slightly pink.

Sadie raises an eyebrow. "Guy stuff, huh? Well, don't let me interrupt. I've got to close up, anyway."

As Sadie moves away, Ren turns to me with a slightly panicked look. "Listen, Arthur, about what I said..."

I hold up a hand. "Don't worry, son. Your secret's safe with me."

Ren visibly relaxes, and we spend the next few minutes in companionable silence, helping Sadie close up the library.

As we step out into the snowy evening, Sadie turns to me. "Will we see you tomorrow, Arthur?"

I nod, feeling a warmth that has nothing to do with the temperature. "Wouldn't miss it for the world."

Ren and Sadie wave goodbye, walking off together, their laughter echoing in the quiet street. I watch them go, more determined than ever to figure out this whole friendship business. I close my eyes, reaching out to Henry like a flower stretching towards the sun.

In a blink, I feel the warmth of the celestial realm. Henry's kind face appears in my mind's eye, his blue eyes twinkling like he knows something I don't. Which he probably does.

"Ah, Arthur," he says, voice echoing in my thoughts. "How goes your first day?"

I sigh, feeling about as qualified for this job as a daisy is for deep-sea diving. "It's... complicated," I admit.

"Human emotions are more tangled than ivy on an old brick wall."

Henry chuckles softly. "Indeed, they are. But that's what makes them beautiful, don't you think?"

I think about Ren and Sadie, about their deep friendship and the unspoken longing between them. "I suppose," I concede, reluctant as a tree losing its leaves. "Although I'm not sure what I'm doing here." I scratch my beard. "Seems like he ought to be teaching me."

"Don't worry. Time will reveal all things," Henry says, gentle as a spring breeze. "You were chosen for this assignment and I know you'll succeed."

I nod and can't help but feel a glimmer of hope after talking to Henry. It's like the first green shoot after winter. "Thanks, Henry. I'll do my best. Even if my best feels about as useful as Rebecca forecasting sunshine during a blizzard right now."

As Henry fades away, I open my eyes, feeling more grounded. I may not have all the answers, but I'm determined to see this through. For Ren, for Sadie, and for my shot at those wings.

I just hope Henry's right and I'll figure out what exactly my assignment is sooner than later.

With a deep breath that fogs up the chilly air, I teleport back to my heavenly home. Time to mull over the day and brace myself for whatever comes next. My mission's only just sprouted, and I've got a feeling it's going to grow into one heck of a Christmas season. Here's hoping I don't need pruning shears to get through it.

I can't help but think about my classmates and wonder how they're doing with their assignments. Are they finding it as challenging and bewildering as I am? I chuckle to myself, imagining Lillian trying to guide lost souls with lollipops or John caroling in his colorful socks.

With that thought, I settle in for the night, ready to tackle whatever tomorrow brings in this strange, wonderful, confusing world of human emotions and friendships. Who knew earning wings would be such a wild ride?

Two

ARTHUR

The town square of Benton Falls unfolds before me like a winter wonderland postcard come to life. Fresh snow blankets the quaint storefronts, transforming the already charming town into a magical scene.

As I stroll through the square, the brisk, invigorating air fills my lungs, carrying with it the mingled scents of pine, cinnamon, and wood smoke. The crunch of snow beneath my feet provides a satisfying rhythm to my walk, while in the distance, I can hear the faint tinkling of sleigh bells and the melodious voices of carolers rehearsing for the upcoming Christmas festival.

Despite the serene beauty surrounding me, my mind is preoccupied with the complexities of my assignment. How am I supposed to help Ren understand the true meaning of friendship when he and Sadie already seem to have such a strong bond? The question weighs on me, heavier than the snow-laden branches of the nearby evergreens.

My wandering gaze lands on Sadie, who's busy hanging garlands across the library windows. Her warm smile and infectious energy seem to brighten the sky. She's perched precariously on a ladder, her tongue peeking out slightly in concentration as she stretches to secure a particularly stubborn piece of greenery.

"Need a hand there, Sadie?" I call out, moving closer to steady the wobbling ladder.

She looks down; her face lighting up with recognition. "Arthur! Good morning! I wouldn't say no to some angelic intervention with these decorations."

Wait, she knows I'm an angel? I'm taken aback. Who told her?

I watch her as she continues to work and then I realize she doesn't know. I chuckle at her choice of words, wondering if she has any idea how close to the truth she is. As I hold the ladder steady, I can't help but feel a sense of reassurance. Sadie's kindness and energy will be crucial in helping me reach Ren, I'm sure of it.

Just as Sadie descends the ladder, our peaceful morning is disrupted by the rumble of a large moving van making its way down the street. I watch curiously as a sandy-haired young man emerges from the van, his green eyes alight with excitement and curiosity as he takes in the town square.

"Oh!" Sadie exclaims, her eyes widening with interest. "That must be the new bookstore owner. I heard he was arriving today."

Before I can respond, Sadie is already making her way towards the newcomer, her natural warmth and friendliness on full display. I follow at a more sedate pace, my angelic senses already picking up on the instant connection forming between them.

"Welcome to Benton Falls!" Sadie calls out, extending her hand. "I'm Sadie Jameson, the town librarian. You must be Ethan?"

The young man's face breaks into a charming grin as he shakes Sadie's hand. "Yes, Ethan Parker."

"You're opening the bookstore?" Sadie grins.

The man nods as he takes in Sadie. "Yes, coming soon, 'The Bookmark's Corner'."

"That's so great. It's always nice to meet another book worm." She chuckles and Ethan seems taken by the girl. Their shared passion for literature sparks a lively exchange, and I can't help but notice how Sadie's eyes light up as they discuss favorite authors and upcoming book releases. Her laughter rings out, a sound that both warms and worries me.

I'm not crazy about this new development, aka Ethan. My assignment with Ren just became a little more complicated.

Speaking of Ren, I spot him approaching from down the street, looking dashing in his police uniform. His face brightens as he sees Sadie. But I detect a subtle flicker of confusion and something else—jealousy, perhaps? — in his eyes as he takes in the animated conversation between Sadie and Ethan.

"Morning, Sades," Ren calls out, joining our little group with a cheerful grin that doesn't quite reach his eyes. "Making new friends already?"

Sadie turns to Ren, her face glowing with excitement. "Ren. Perfect timing. This is Ethan Parker. He's opening the new bookstore in town. Ethan, this is Ren Micahels, Benton Falls' finest police officer and my best friend since... well, forever!"

I watch closely as Ren and Ethan shake hands, noting the slightly firmer than necessary grip from both men. Ren's smile remains in place, but there's a new tension in his shoulders that wasn't there before.

"Welcome to Benton Falls," Ren says, his tone friendly but with an undercurrent of something I can't quite place. "I'm sure you'll love it here. It's a great community."

Ethan nods enthusiastically. "I can already tell. Everyone's been so welcoming, and the town is just beautiful. I can't wait to get the store up and running."

"Oh!" Sadie exclaims, clapping her hands together. "I'd love to help you set up. Maybe we could organize a grand opening event? Partner with the library for a reading or something?"

Ethan's face lights up at the suggestion. "That would be fantastic. I was hoping to tap into your expertise. Maybe we could grab coffee sometime and brainstorm ideas?"

I notice Ren stiffen slightly at this, his smile becoming a bit forced. "Sounds like you two will have a lot to talk about," he says, his voice carefully neutral. "Sadie's the best when it comes to all things, books and community events."

Sadie beams at the compliment, oblivious to the

undercurrent of tension. "Thanks, Ren. Oh. We should all have dinner together once Ethan's settled in. Show him some true Benton Falls hospitality."

As Sadie and Ethan continue to chat enthusiastically about books and potential collaborations, I observe Ren's reactions carefully. He's trying his best to appear interested and welcoming, but I can sense the conflicting emotions roiling beneath his calm exterior. It's clear that Ethan's arrival has thrown a wrench into the delicate balance of Ren and Sadie's relationship.

Eventually, Ethan excuses himself to continue unloading the moving van, and Sadie turns to Ren with shining eyes. "Isn't this exciting? A new bookstore in town! It'll be so good for the community."

Ren nods, his smile not quite reaching his eyes. "Yeah, it's great. Listen, Sades, I was wondering if you wanted to grab lunch later? Maybe at Molly's Diner?"

"Oh, I'd love to," Sadie says, her face falling slightly. "But I promised Mrs. Hathaway I'd help with the children's story time at the library today. Rain check?"

"Sure, no problem," Ren says, his disappointment clear to me, if not to Sadie. "Maybe tomorrow?"

Sadie nods enthusiastically. "Definitely. Oh, I should get back to decorating. See you later, Ren."

As Sadie hurries back to the library, Ren stands there for a moment, watching her go with a wistful expression. I decide it's time to make my presence known again.

"She's quite something, isn't she?" I say, moving to stand beside Ren.

He starts slightly, as if he'd forgotten I was there. "Yeah, she is," he agrees, his voice soft. "Sadie's... special."

I nod sagely. "You two seem very close."

Ren's face softens into a genuine smile, a flicker of hope in his eyes before it's quickly extinguished. "Like I told you yesterday, Sadie and I... we're just friends."

I can sense the lie in his words, the fear and uncertainty behind them. It's becoming clearer to me now— my assignment isn't just about helping Ren understand friendship, but perhaps helping him find the courage to risk that friendship for something deeper.

As Ren excuses himself to start his patrol, I'm left alone in the town square, pondering the challenges that lie ahead. Ethan's arrival has added a new layer of complexity to an already delicate situation. While I'm happy that Sadie has found a kindred spirit in her love for literature, I worry about the strain it might put on her bond with Ren.

That night, just outside my little mansion in the sky, I tend to the blooms in my garden. I carefully trim an angel's trumpet flower, its delicate petals reminding me of the fragile nature of human relationships. How can I strengthen the bond between Sadie and Ren while ensuring it remains strong, despite Ethan's unintentional interference? I'm determined not to fail my final task, but the path forward seems as tangled as the vines of my celestial morning glories.

Stripping off my gardening gloves, I gaze up at the heavens, seeking divine inspiration. A shooting star streaks across the night sky, filling me with a sense of hope and determination. As if on cue, I feel the comforting presence of Henry, my mentor.

"Ah, Arthur," Henry's warm voice fills my mind. "How did things go today?"

I sigh, running a hand through my beard. "It's... complicated, Henry. Ren and Sadie already have a strong friendship, but there's something more there that they're both afraid to acknowledge. And now there's this new fellow, Ethan, who seems to be throwing things off balance."

Henry chuckles softly. "The course of true love never did run smooth, as they say. But remember, Arthur, your task is to help Ren understand the true spirit of friendship. Sometimes, that means having the courage to risk that friendship for something deeper."

I nod slowly, mulling over his words. "I figured that had something to do with my assignment."

"You're beginning to understand," Henry says, his voice filled with pride. "Trust in your instincts, Arthur. You have more wisdom to offer than you realize."

"I hope you're right." I sigh, wishing I felt as confident. I was the last angel to be advising anyone on relationships. Did Henry know how I struggled to make friends or that I never married during my time on earth?

Henry laughs again as his presence fades and I can't help but smile.

Of course he does.

Three

REN

I'm striding down Main Street, my reindeer sweater barely keeping out the December chill. My mind's racing: *Come on, Ren. You're a cop. You chase bad guys for a living. A gingerbread contest is no big deal. It's not like I'm a rookie on his first beat.*

The community center looms ahead, looking like Santa's workshop after an extreme makeover. I push open the doors and BAM!—the aroma of gingerbread nearly knocks me over.

I scan the room, looking for Sadie and see Arthur on the opposite side of the center, watching the professionals at work as they create Architectural Digest masterpieces out of baking goods. I turn back to the amateur section and locate Sadie. There she is, focused on her gingerbread creation like she's defusing a bomb. Her thick hair is pulled back except for the rebellious loose strands falling around her face, and I swear, even from here, I can see that cute little frown she gets when she's concentrating. My heart does its usual Sadie-induced acrobatics. I make a mental note to get my cholesterol checked. This can't be healthy.

I saunter over, aiming for "cool and collected" but probably looking more like I'm casing the joint. Ever since I admitted to myself how I really feel about Sadie, I've been acting stupid. "Hey, Sadie," I call out.

Sadie looks up, flashing a smile that could melt permafrost. "Ren! I was thinking you'd gotten a call about a donut shop robbery on the way here."

I clutch my chest, playing wounded. "Low blow, Sades. I'll have you know I passed two donut shops to get here on time. That's practically heroic."

She laughs, the sound doing things to my insides that I'm pretty sure violate the laws of physics. "Your medal is the honor of being my gingerbread architect partner. Now grab a piping bag, tough guy. These walls aren't gonna frost themselves."

Reaching for my apron, the one covered in little Santa's dressed as police officers, the same one I use every year, I shake my head. "I can't believe you started without me. And here I thought this year you were trying to move up from the amateur to the pro division? How are you supposed to do that without your lead architect?"

Sadie stops and points to the man on the other side of the room, the one behind the camera filming the Ramirez family constructing their winning entry. "I had to get an early start. Did you know they're televising the gingerbread competition on national news station?"

"I heard something about that." I look over at the

TV crew—all 3 of them — as the reporter comments on how the Ramirez entry wins every year. "How big of a deal can it be? The network sent 3 people?"

Sadie chuckles. "I guess you're right. Better not get distracted by the bright lights of Hollywood."

As we start working, I can't help but notice how in sync we are, like we're executing a well-planned stake-out. I'm about to make a smooth comment about our team-work when a voice that could charm Frosty back to life interrupts us.

"Well, well, if it isn't Benton Falls' finest." Ethan's approaching, looking like he just stepped out of a Christmas catalog. I resist the urge to frisk him for hidden hair product. "I hope you're ready for some serious competition, because I've got a few tricks up my sleeve."

"Yeah?" I shoot back. "Is one of those tricks making a gingerbread house that doesn't look like it was hit by a SWAT team?"

Sadie elbows me, but I catch the smile she's trying to hide. Ethan, to his credit, laughs it off. "Touché, Officer. May the best builder win!"

As the contest kicks into high gear, I find myself more focused on Sadie and Ethan than I am on the gingerbread house. Ethan's busy regaling Sadie with tales of his college gingerbread disasters. I wrack my brain for a comeback. "Hey Sadie," I say, "remember that time in high school when we tried to make a gingerbread house, and it looked like it had been through police academy training?"

Sadie snorts, nearly dropping her piping bag. "Oh man, how could I forget? We used so much frosting trying to hold it together, it looked like a sugar-coated disaster zone!"

"Mrs. Henderson still put it on display in the library," I remind her. "Right next to the 'How Not to Decorate' poster. Fitting, really."

We're both cracking up, and for a moment, it's just us in our little bubble of shared history and inside jokes. But then I notice Arthur watching us. He's got this mischievous look that makes me wonder if he's got some mistletoe in his back pocket.

Suddenly, there's a commotion at Ethan's station. His icing bowl has mysteriously tipped over, creating a winter wonderland in his workspace. As Ethan rushes off to clean up, Arthur swoops in to help, then turns to us with some gingerbread wisdom.

As we work on our candy cane shingles, following Arthur's advice, Sadie and I fall into our usual rhythm. We're trading quips and terrible puns faster than I can read a perp of his rights.

"Hey Ren," Sadie says, her eyes gleaming with mischief, "what do you call a snowman with a six-pack?"

I groan, bracing myself. "I don't know, Sadie. What?"

"An abdominal snowman!"

I roll my eyes so hard I'm surprised I don't pull a muscle. "That was terrible. You should be ashamed of yourself."

"Oh yeah? Let's see you do better, Officer Wiseguy."

I clear my throat, channeling my inner stand-up

comedian. "What do you call a cat on the beach at Christmas time?"

Sadie narrows her eyes. "I'm afraid to ask."

"Sandy Claws!"

She groans, but she's laughing too. "That's it. You're officially banned from making puns for the rest of the night."

"Can't handle the heat, huh?" I retort, flicking a bit of powdered sugar at her.

For a brief, shining moment, everything feels right in the world. It's just me and Sadie, bantering like we've done a thousand times before. I can almost forget about Ethan and his perfect hair and his charming smile and his probably not-at-all-suspicious bookstore.

But then Ethan returns. He's back to complimenting Sadie's icing work, and I'm back to feeling like I'm working crowd control at a two-person party.

As I add a couple more shingles, I overhear Ethan inviting Sadie to his bookstore opening. My stomach does a free-fall that would make a skydiver jealous. I try to focus on our gingerbread house, but my brain is too busy coming up with increasingly ridiculous scenarios. Maybe I could convince the Chief to raid the bookstore for contraband literature. Or I could challenge Ethan to a snowball duel at dawn. People still do that, right?

Despite our best efforts—and my internal crisis—I'm worried our gingerbread house will lose to a replica of the town clock tower. I'm pretty sure I see the clock tower hands actually moving, which seems like cheating to me, but I resist the urge to call for backup.

Arthur materializes at my elbow like he's been taking stealth lessons from Santa. "You know," he says, his voice low and conspiratorial, "I hear the Sweet Haven Bakery and Cafe makes hot chocolate so good, it could make a hardened criminal confess."

I blink, wondering if I've somehow picked up a Christmas guardian angel with questionable intentions. But hey, I'm not one to turn down an invitation for hot chocolate.

"Hey Sadie," I say, channeling every ounce of cool I've got—which isn't much—"want to drown our gingerbread sorrows in some liquid chocolate therapy?"

Sadie's face lights up, brightening my universe. "Ren, that's the best idea you've had all night. Let's roll."

As we walk to the cafe, the snow falls, turning Benton Falls into a living Christmas card. I have a sudden urge to grab Sadie's hand and pull her close, like we're in some cheesy holiday movie. Instead, I shove my hands deeper into my pockets and say, "So, you think if we ate enough snow, we'd eventually turn into abominable snowmen?"

Sadie laughs, the sound crystal clear in the quiet night. "Only you would think about the tactical advantages of becoming a snow monster, Ren."

"Hey, I'm just planning ahead. Climate change is real, Sadie. We might need to adapt our pursuit techniques."

The Sweet Haven Bakery and Cafe is like stepping into a warm interrogation room, minus the one-way mirror. We snag a booth by the window, and soon we're

27

sipping hot chocolates that make my taste buds want to confess to crimes they didn't even commit.

"Remember that time in middle school when you got your tongue stuck to that metal pole?" Sadie asks, her eyes twinkling with barely contained laughter.

I groan, feeling the phantom pain. "Don't remind me. I still have nightmares about being permanently attached to that pole, forced to direct traffic with my eyebrows for the rest of my life."

Sadie's laughing so hard she nearly snorts hot chocolate out of her nose. "Your face was priceless! You looked like a very confused, very cold, angry bulldog."

"Yeah, yeah, laugh it up," I grumble, but I'm grinning too. "Just remember, I've got enough dirt on you to fill a case file, missy. Or should I bring up the Great Banana Peel Incident of 2010?"

Sadie gasps in mock horror. "You wouldn't dare!"

"Try me, Sadie. I've got the witness statements to back it up."

As we trade stories and laugh at shared memories, I feel that proverbial ache in my chest. It's like my heart is trying to bust out of jail, but it's stuck behind my ribs. I want this—Sadie's laughter, her warmth, the way she gets me like no one else does. But then there's Ethan and the way she seems taken by him and his books. Add my own fear, and suddenly I feel like I'm defusing a bomb with no training.

All too soon, it's time to head home. We stand outside the cafe, and I swear the snowflakes falling around Sadie make her look like she's in her own personal snow globe. For a moment, I think I see something in her eyes—a flicker of something more. But then she blinks, and it's gone, and I'm left wondering if I imagined the whole thing.

"Thanks for tonight, Ren," she says softly. "I needed this."

"Anytime, Sades," I reply, trying to ignore the way my heart is doing the cha-cha in my chest. "That's what partners are for, right? Gingerbread construction, hot chocolate therapy, and terrible puns."

She laughs and gives me a quick hug before turning to walk towards her apartment. I watch her go, feeling like I'm in one of those cheesy Hallmark movies where the guy always chokes at the last minute.

As I trudge home, my thoughts are a jumbled mess of Sadie, Ethan, and enough emotional baggage to unpack over a lifetime. The Christmas lights twinkling on every house seem to taunt me. "Hey Ren," they seem to say, "why don't you man up and tell the girl how you feel? Also, your reindeer sweater violates at least three fashion laws."

I'm so lost in my thoughts that I almost miss Arthur standing near my front porch. He turns as I approach, his blue eyes twinkling like he's got insider information on a big case.

"Quite an evening, wasn't it?" he says, his voice warm and somehow familiar. "You know, young man, sometimes the greatest risks bring the greatest rewards. But it takes courage to take that first step."

Before I can ask him if he's moonlighting as a fortune

cookie writer, he's gone, swallowed up by the gently falling snow. I'm left standing there, wondering if I've just been given life advice by a hallucination brought on by too much sugar and emotional stress.

I trudge up the steps to my front door and go inside, my brain helpfully supplying a montage of every awkward moment from the evening set to the theme from COPS. As I get ready for bed, my eyes fall on a framed photo of Sadie and me from last Christmas. We're both laughing, cheeks rosy from the cold, looking disgustingly happy and couple-y despite not actually being a couple.

I flop onto my bed, staring at the ceiling and wondering if it's too late to ask Santa for "the guts to tell your best friend you're in love with her without making a complete idiot of yourself" for Christmas.

As I drift off to sleep, my last coherent thought is: *Maybe I should have just become a gingerbread man. Seems like a much simpler life. No emotions, no complications... just the constant fear of being eaten.*

The last thing I see before sleep claims me is Sadie's smile, bright and beautiful, forever just out of reach. But hey, at least in my dreams, I can pretend I'm smooth enough to actually do something about it.

A guy can dream, right?

Four

REN

I push open the heavy oak doors of the Evergreen Library, my police uniform crisp and freshly pressed. The recognizable scent of books and dust hits me like a warm hug from an old friend. It's as comforting as my favorite coffee mug and just as likely to keep me up at night overthinking things.

My eyes scan the room, automatically searching for Sadie. I spot her behind a mountain of books that would make even the most seasoned librarian break out in a cold sweat. She's elbow-deep in wrapping paper, her brow furrowed as she concentrates on her task.

"Well, well," I call out, approaching her desk. "Looks like I've stumbled upon a crime scene. Death by literature?"

Sadie looks up, her hazel eyes sparkling with that particular brand of holiday cheer that makes my heart jingle all the way. "Officer Michaels. To what do we owe

31

this official visit? Did someone report a missing bookmark?"

I grin, tipping my hat. "Just doing my civic duty, ma'am. Heard there was a disturbance involving paper cuts and excessive holiday spirit."

She laughs, the sound making me feel warmer than my kevlar vest. "Well, you're just in time to join the chaos. We're wrapping books for the hotel's Sub for Santa program. Every kid in Benton Falls is getting a book to unwrap on Christmas morning."

My chest swells with a mix of pride and affection. Leave it to Sadie to turn the library into Santa's literary workshop. "Alright then, where do you want me, boss? I've got handcuff experience that translates surprisingly well to ribbon-tying."

As I unbutton my uniform jacket—mentally high-fiving myself for remembering to iron my shirt this morning—Arthur appears from around the corner.

"Ah, Benton Falls' finest!" he says. There's a twinkle in his eyes that seems to get brighter every time I see him, which I swear wasn't there the day I met him. But then again, hanging around Sadie has that effect on people. "Here to protect and serve... our wrapping station?"

For the next hour, we fall into a comfortable rhythm. Arthur guides Sadie through the finer points of corner-folding, while I handle each book like it's a fragile antique. The quiet intimacy of the moment isn't lost on me. It's like we're in our own little bubble, just me, Sadie, and our enigmatic Santa-lookalike friend.

I'm just about to make a smooth comment about

how well we work together—you know, as friends... totally platonic book-wrapping buddies — when the library doors burst open with all the subtlety of an FBI raid.

"Ho ho ho, fellow book lovers. I'm here to help prepare for the book fair."

And just like that, our cozy bubble pops. Ethan breezes in, his eyes light up when he sees Sadie and a wide smile spreads across his face. He plops down next to Sadie, who's suddenly looking at him like he's the last cookie in the jar.

I suppress an eye roll so hard I'm pretty sure I strain something. My jaw tightens as Ethan launches into a barrage of literary banter and holiday puns that have Sadie doubling over in laughter.

"Hey Sadie," Ethan grins, leaning in close enough that I can practically see the sparkle of his teeth. "What do you call a broke Santa Claus? St. Nickel-less!"

Sadie snorts, nearly dropping the book she's wrapping. "Oh man, that's terrible! Okay, okay, I've got one. Why don't mountains read? Because they prefer cliff notes!"

As their laughter mingles in the air, I feel something in my chest tighten. It's like watching my partner get all the credit for cracking a case I've been working on for years.

"Well," I say, standing up abruptly and nearly knocking over a stack of children's books, "I should probably get going. Streets to patrol, you know. Can't let the snowmen get up to any mischief."

Sadie looks up at me, her smile fading slightly. "Oh, already? But we've still got so many books to wrap..."

I force a grin that feels about as natural as a toupee on a cat. "Duty calls, Sades. But hey, you've got Ethan here to pick up my slack. I'm sure he's a pro at wrapping... things."

As I head for the door, adjusting my uniform hat, I notice Arthur shifting closer to Sadie, his voice carrying louder than necessary as he asks her opinion on different wrapping techniques. It's a clumsy attempt to redirect her attention from Ethan's dazzling smile, but I appreciate the effort.

The chilly winter air hits me as I step outside, clearing my head a bit. I take a deep breath, the scent of pine and wood smoke filling my lungs. As I stand on the steps, my thoughts are as tangled as Christmas lights after a year in storage.

I know Arthur's trying to help me connect with Sadie. Heck, I know I should be in there right now, not out here sulking like a rookie who got assigned parking duty. But seeing Ethan sweep in with his perfect hair and his witty banter... it's more than I can watch.

My brooding is interrupted by a tug on my uniform sleeve. I look down to see a little girl, her cheeks as rosy as Rudolph's nose, gazing up at me with wide eyes.

"Officer Ren," she says solemnly, "what books do you think Santa likes best? I want to leave one out with his cookies this year."

Just like that, my mood lifts. I crouch down to her level, pretending to give her question a serious thought.

"Well, now that's a very important question. I think Santa probably enjoys a good mystery. After all, he has to figure out who's been naughty or nice all year."

The little girl nods sagely, like I've just imparted the wisdom of the ages. As she scampers off to tell her mom about Santa's literary preferences, I feel a renewed sense of purpose.

I may not have Ethan's charm or his way with words, but I've got something he doesn't—a history with Sadie, and a deep connection to this town and its people. And maybe, just maybe, that's enough.

As I look back towards the library doors, I glimpse Sadie through the window. She's laughing at something Arthur said. Her face lit up with joy. And in that moment, I know I'm not giving up. Whatever it takes, I'm going to be the steady force in her life, the friend she can always count on.

And who knows? Maybe someday, that friendship will bloom into something more. After all, strange things have happened in Benton Falls. Like, the time Mrs. Henderson's cat got elected to the town council. But that's a story for another day.

For now, I've got a town to protect and a friendship to nurture. And if I happen to accidentally lock Ethan in the library overnight... well, that's just me doing my job, right?

Five

ARTHUR

I n the back pew of the Benton Falls Church, my earthly form settling onto the worn wood with a soft creak. The air is thick with the mingled scents of evergreen and melting wax, a heady combination that reminds me of celestial gardens and starlit nights. It's Sunday evening, and the church is buzzing with anticipation for the choir's Christmas performance.

As I scan the crowd, my angelic senses pick up on the swirling emotions filling the space. There's excitement, nervousness, and... ah, there it is. The complicated tangle of feelings I've come to associate with Ren and Sadie. Speaking of which...

I watch fondly as Sadie files in with the choir, the warm hues of her hair gleaming under the soft glow of candlelight. She looks radiant; her face alight with the joy of music and the spirit of the season. My heart swells with a mix of pride and affection. In the short time I've known her, Sadie embodies everything I believe a human should be - kind, generous, and full of love.

Moments later, Ren slips into the church, his police uniform crisp and sharp. I can't help but chuckle to myself. If only he knew how much that uniform reminded me of less-than-stellar moments in my earthly life. But those days are long behind me, and now I'm here to help this good-hearted officer find his way.

I catch the soft look that passes between Ren and Sadie, a moment of connection that speaks volumes about their shared history and deep bond. But then Ren's gaze is drawn to the entrance, where Ethan appears, looking dapper in a suit that probably costs more than my entire heavenly wardrobe. Not *that we really have those up there, but you get the idea.*

As the first soaring notes of "O Holy Night" ring out, I settle in to observe the drama unfolding before me. On stage, all is serene beauty and holiday cheer. But beneath the surface? It's more turbulent than the time I accidentally over watered the celestial cactus garden.

Ren's eyes drift wistfully to Sadie, his jaw tightening imperceptibly as he watches her sing. I can practically see the words he wants to say floating above his head like those thought bubbles in comic strips. "You're beautiful," they'd say. "I love you." But he remains silent, his emotions locked away tighter than the pearly gates.

When the choir transitions into a sprightly carol, I decide it's time for a little angelic intervention. Covertly, I channel my celestial energy, weaving an invisible thread of harmony between Sadie and Ren's parts. Their voices blend in perfect synchronicity, a musical representation of the connection they share.

For a fleeting moment, the magic works its wonders. Sadie and Ren share a private smile, their connection a shining beacon amidst the scripted festivity of the performance. I allow myself a smug grin. Not bad for a former gardener, eh?

But just as I'm about to pat myself on the back— *metaphorically, of course* - the spell is swiftly shattered. Ethan, with all the subtlety of a neon sign in heaven, mouths "beautiful" at Sadie with an admiring gaze. Her cheeks flush prettily, and I can practically hear the sound of Ren's heart sinking.

I grimace as Ren's shoulders slump, his confidence deflating faster than a punctured tire. Oh, Ren. If only you could see what I see—the way Sadie's eyes always find you first, the way her smile brightens when you're near. But love, it seems, can make even the most observant humans blind.

During the rousing handbell finale, I make one last desperate attempt to regain the mood. Using my angelic powers—*and feeling a bit like a cosmic puppeteer*—I try to sync Sadie and Ren's movements. It's like I'm pulling invisible strings, trying to make these two stubborn humans dance to the tune of true love.

But alas, even heavenly intervention has its limits. Ren fumbles his part, nearly dropping his handbell as he shoots a cutting glare at Ethan's smugly grinning face. Sadie freezes, panic glazing her eyes as she realizes how thoroughly Ethan has shaken Ren's usual easy grace.

As the performance ends and the congregation breaks into applause, I hang back, observing the aftermath of this emotional rollercoaster. The choir files out, heading to the church basement for a celebratory gathering. But Ren... oh, poor Ren. His face is a mask of pain as he abruptly turns and flees the church, looking for all the world like a man running from his own heart.

I see Ethan notice Ren's hasty exit, a flicker of concern crossing his face. He moves to follow, but I'm quicker. With a bit of angelic maneuvering (and perhaps a strategically placed hymnal or two), I manage to block his path. Ren needs privacy right now, space to wrestle with the fear that's threatening to overwhelm him.

As Ethan gets waylaid by a group of admiring choir members (honestly, the man could charm the halo off an angel), I slip out of the church, following the trail of Ren's turbulent emotions. I find him in the church basement, slumped against the wall, cradling his head in his hands.

My heart—the celestial version—breaks as I watch Ren's deepest vulnerability bubble to the surface. The terror of abandonment he's harbored since childhood, the fear that everyone he loves will eventually leave him. It all comes pouring out in silent, shuddering breaths.

I want nothing more than to reach out, to offer some words of comfort or wisdom. But I know that's not my role right now. Sometimes, the most important thing we can do is simply bear witness to someone's pain, to hold space for their grief and fear.

As I watch Ren struggle with his emotions, I'm

struck by a sudden, overwhelming wave of empathy. It's more intense than anything I've felt before, even in my celestial training. Is this what Henry meant when he said this mission would change me? That by helping humans understand friendship and love, I might come to understand them better myself?

With a weary sigh, I retreat to the celestial realm to regather my strength. As the earthly plane fades away and heaven's glow envelops me, I can't shake the image of Ren's anguished face from my mind.

I find myself in my favorite spot in the celestial gardens, surrounded by blooming jasmine and starlit roses. But even the beauty of paradise feels dimmed compared to the raw, powerful emotions I witnessed on Earth.

"Tough day at the office, Arthur?"

I turn to see Henry approaching, his silver hair gleaming in the soft heavenly light. His eyes twinkle with understanding, and I'm once again struck by how much wisdom and compassion he carries.

"Henry," I greet him, my voice heavy with the weight of my experiences. "I... I don't know if I'm cut out for this. Guiding humans through love and friendship? It's more complicated than cultivating a garden of temperamental orchids."

Henry chuckles, settling down beside me on a cloud-like bench. "Ah, but that's the beauty of it, my friend. Love, friendship, orchids — they all require patience, care, and a willingness to get your hands dirty."

I sigh, running a hand through my beard. "But

Henry, I thought my job was to help Ren and Sadie become more than friends. Now I'm not so sure. Watching Ren suffer... it's heartbreaking. Not sure it's worth it."

Henry's eyes soften with understanding. "Arthur, your assignment isn't about forcing a specific outcome. It's about helping Ren understand the true spirit of friendship. Sometimes, that means watching those we care about struggle and grow."

"But how can I just stand by and watch him hurt?" I ask, frustration coloring my voice. "Isn't there more I could do?"

Henry places a comforting hand on my shoulder. "By being there, by caring, you're already doing more than you know. Remember, we can't interfere with free will. Ren and Sadie must make their own choices. Your job is to guide, to illuminate the path, not to walk it for them."

I nod slowly, letting his words sink in. "I just... I've never felt empathy like this before, Henry. It's overwhelming." I sigh. "Maybe there's a reason I avoided it on earth."

A smile spreads across Henry's face, warm and proud. "As you help humans understand love and friendship, you too will grow in understanding. This empathy you're feeling? It's shaping you into the guardian angel you're meant to be."

As Henry's words wash over me, I feel a renewed sense of purpose stirring in my celestial being. Yes, this assignment is challenging. Yes, it's pushing me far beyond my comfort zone of tending heavenly gardens. But maybe that's exactly what I need.

"Thank you, Henry," I say, feeling a bit more centered. "I think I'm ready to go back now."

Henry nods, his eyes twinkling. "Remember, Arthur. In matters of the heart, sometimes the most powerful thing we can do is simply be present. Your empathy, your care—that's the true magic of being a guardian angel."

With those words echoing in my mind, I prepare to return to Earth. As I feel the accustomed pull of gravity, I make a silent promise to Ren, to Sadie, and to myself. I may not have all the answers, but I'll be there, a steady presence in the storm of emotions they're navigating.

After all, isn't that what friendship is truly about? Being there, through the high notes and the fumbled handbells, through the stolen glances and the unspoken words. As I reappear in the earthly realm, I feel a new determination coursing through me.

This guardian angel in training is just getting started.

Six

REN

I sit on the edge of my bed, staring blankly at the wall like it's a one-way mirror in an interrogation room. My house feels emptier than a donut box after a night shift, the silence pressing down on me harder than a perp resisting arrest. The Christmas lights I halfheartedly strung up last week mock me with their cheerful twinkle, a stark contrast to the gloom settling in my chest.

Suddenly, there's a knock at the door. For a split second, my heart does a somersault, hoping it might be Sadie. I hustle over and turn the handle. As I open the door, my enthusiasm is on the run, when it isn't Sadie's face looking back at me.

There stands Arthur, looking like Santa Claus decided to moonlight as a therapist. His kind eyes twinkle with concern, and I swear I catch a whiff of pine and cinnamon wafting off him. It's oddly comforting, like Christmas spirit in human form.

"Rough night, son?" he asks, his voice as warm as a fresh cup of cocoa.

I nod, swallowing hard against the lump in my throat. "I can't lose her, Arthur," I admit, my voice cracking like ice on a spring thaw and I can' t believe I'm saying so much. "Sadie is the one constant good thing I have left after my parents' divorce tore our family apart."

Arthur steps inside, and we sit down on the couch. I clutch a throw pillow to my chest like it's a bulletproof vest, protecting my heart from the barrage of emotions threatening to break through.

"Tell me about it," Arthur says gently, and suddenly, it's like someone's opened the floodgates.

I unravel painful memories—my father's emotional abandonment, colder than a January night in Benton Falls. My mother's bitterness, poisoning every interaction like a toxic spill. Arthur listens intently, his calm presence encouraging me to continue, like a seasoned detective coaxing out a witness statement.

"I watched that hostility destroy any chance at an amicable split," I choke out, feeling like I'm confessing to a crime I didn't commit. "I can't go through that again with Sadie."

My hands clench into fists as I hug the throw pillow tighter, my knuckles whitening like I'm holding onto the last shred of hope. "Our friendship means more to me than any romantic love. I won't risk tainting it."

Arthur's brow furrows, creating more wrinkles than a map of Benton Falls' back roads. "But Ren," he says gently, "your situation with Sadie is entirely different.

You two have a foundation of friendship and mutual respect. That's not something that easily crumbles."

I shake my head. "You don't understand, Arthur. I've seen how love can turn bitter. How affection can breed resentment faster than mold on forgotten evidence. I can't risk that with Sadie. She's... she's everything."

Arthur sighs, a sound that seems to carry the weight of centuries. "I understand your fear, Ren. But love isn't always a battlefield, you know. Sometimes it's a garden that needs tending."

I snort, a sound caught between a laugh and a sob. "Yeah, well, I've never been much of a gardener. More of a bull in a China shop when it comes to relationships."

Arthur pats my shoulder, his touch as light as a snowflake but somehow grounding. "You might surprise yourself, Ren. The heart has a way of growing, even in the harshest conditions."

As Arthur leaves, I'm left with a strange mix of comfort and confusion. It's like being wrapped in a warm blanket while standing in a blizzard—cozy, but still facing a storm.

The next day, I'm on patrol, but my mind's anywhere but on the job. I feel like I'm sleepwalking through my rounds, my usual calm demeanor as forced as a smile in a mugshot. The festive decorations around town seem to mock me, their cheer a stark contrast to the melancholy hanging over me like a rain cloud.

Later, I find myself at the library, drawn there like a moth to a flame. Or more accurately, like a lovesick idiot to the girl who holds his heart. Sadie's there, of course, looking beautiful in a soft green sweater that makes her eyes shine like Christmas lights.

I hoped Sadie hadn't noticed how I let Ethan's presence get to me the other night, but I should've known better. There seems to be some silent understanding between us as we maintain a careful distance, exchanging stilted pleasantries that mask our yearning for the easy cadence now tarnished by my hasty exit from the church. It's like we're reading from a script, our usual banter replaced by dialogue as wooden as a nutcracker.

"How's... how's the holiday reading program going?" I ask, fumbling for words like I'm searching for my handcuffs in the dark.

Sadie nods, her smile not quite reaching her eyes. "Good, good. The kids are really excited about the prize for most books read."

"That's... that's great," I reply, feeling about as eloquent as a parking ticket.

Suddenly, a book slips from Sadie's hands, landing with a thud that seems to echo in the quiet library. We both reach for it at the same time, our hands brushing. Our eyes meet briefly, and I'm hit with a wave of emotion so strong it nearly knocks me off my feet. I handed her the hardbound classic.

"Thanks," she says, clutching the book to her chest. I see in Sadie's eyes the same sorrow that's been gnawing at me, and it's both a comfort and a torture to know she feels it too.

"You're welcome," I answer, wishing I could say so much more. We smile and go back to our familiar roles of longtime friends. I don't know how or when to tell her how I feel about her, or even if I should.

As I leave the library, I play the moment over and over in my mind, the feel of her skin on mine and the heat rushing through my body.

There's no denying it.

I'm crazy about this girl.

Back at home, later that night, I pore over old photo albums, tracing the joyful moments of my parents' happier days before the divorce hurricane struck. It's like looking at evidence from a cold case, searching for clues I might have missed.

I come across a photo that stops me in my tracks. It's from a Christmas years ago, before everything fell apart. We're all there—Mom, Dad, me, and my sister—gathered around the tree. Despite the tensions I now know were simmering beneath the surface, there's genuine joy in our faces. Peace reigning despite their flaws.

As I cradle this snapshot of happier times, I feel something shift inside me. A flicker of hope sparks within—a reminder that love can withstand storms if given root. Maybe, just maybe, Arthur's right. Maybe love isn't always a battlefield. Maybe sometimes, it's worth the risk.

I set the photo down and reach for my phone, my heart pounding like I'm about to storm a suspect's hideout. But instead of calling for backup, I'm calling Sadie.

"Hey, Sades," I say when she picks up, my voice steadier than I feel. "I was wondering... would you like to go ice skating tomorrow? For old times' sake?"

Her answer, warm and eager, floods me with a hope as bright as the star on top of a Christmas tree. As I hang up, I can't help but smile. Maybe I'm not ready to spill my guts just yet, but this... this feels like a start.

I glance at the photo of my family one more time before tucking it away. Love might be a risk, but as I've learned on the job, sometimes the biggest risks lead to the most rewarding outcomes. And Sadie? She's worth every risk in the world.

As I get ready for bed, I catch sight of myself in the mirror. For the first time in days, I look like a man with a mission rather than a lost puppy. "Alright, Michaels," I mutter to my reflection. "Time to cowboy up and show Sadie what she means to you."

I fall asleep, thinking about Sadie on the ice, maybe tripping and falling into my arms—*I wonder if there's an angel hotline to call for some divine intervention.* Smiling, I see Sadie's beautiful face in my mind and think *if I can keep the peace in this town, surely I can win the heart of the girl I love.*

Seven

REN

I'm hunched over my desk at the police station, as focused as a kid in a toy aisle—my mind jumping from shelf to shelf—Sadie... work... Sadie... work. The harsh fluorescent lights buzz overhead, a jarring contrast to the twinkling decorations I can see through the window. My mind's spinning, swirling faster than a suspect fleeing the scene, and I'm struggling to focus on the paperwork in front of me.

The station is quieter than usual today, most of my colleagues out on patrol or enjoying their day off. The only sounds are the gentle hum of computers and the occasional ring of a distant phone. I've been staring at the same report for the past hour, the words blurring together as my thoughts keep drifting back to Sadie and our moment in the library.

Suddenly, Arthur strolls in, looking like Santa collecting the naughty list. His presence is a welcome distraction from the mental hurdles I've been jumping all morning. I glance up, pretty sure my deep blue eyes are as stormy as my thoughts are .

"How's it going, Officer Michaels?" Arthur asks, his calm voice immediately makes me feel a little more at ease.

I sigh, running a hand through my hair. "Good, I guess. I'm just... mulling over this whole Sadie situation."

Arthur settles into the chair across from me, looking for all the world like he's ready for a long interrogation. "I'm listening," he says gently.

Without preamble, I launch into recounting my latest encounter with Sadie at the library. My voice catches as I describe how luminous she looked, gently straightening the crooked book spines.

"She treats those books like they're precious children," I murmur wistfully before clearing my throat, my complexion reddening as I realize I've revealed too much tenderness. "I mean, uh, she's very... dedicated to her job."

I push away from my desk and pace the floor. The linoleum squeaks under my boots, a counterpoint to my restless thoughts. "I tried keeping things casual, you know? But then our fingers touched when I helped her pick up a book she dropped. And it felt like... more."

Arthur watches me with those twinkling blue eyes of his, and I swear I can see the moment realization dawns on his face. That split-second of contact sent Sadie mixed signals. Her hazel eyes had widened in surprise before she averted her gaze, and I'd felt like I'd just fumbled a major piece of evidence.

"I wanted to pull her close, open my heart, but then I retreated like a coward," I mutter darkly, feeling the weight of self-recrimination settle on my shoulders like a lead vest. "Although I called her and asked her to go ice skating."

Arthur leans forward, a hint of excitement or could that be pride in his voice?. "You asked her out?" He grins. "That shows you're trying. Give yourself some credit, Ren."

I stop pacing, letting out a breath I didn't realize I was holding. "Yeah, I guess you're right. It's just... this feels bigger than any case I've ever worked on. The stakes are higher."

Arthur's eyes twinkle with mischief. "Well, Officer, I'd say it's time to gather your evidence and make your move. You've got a date on the ice tonight, don't you?"

I nod, feeling a mix of excitement and terror that's more potent than any adrenaline rush I've ever experienced on the job. "Yeah, I do. Thanks, Arthur. I don't know why, but talking to you always seems to help."

As Arthur leaves, I turn back to my paperwork with renewed focus. I've got a mission tonight, and I intend to see it through.

The rest of my shift crawls by at a snail's pace. Every tick of the clock seems to echo in the quiet office, counting down the minutes until I can see Sadie again. I throw myself into my work, determined to clear my desk before I leave. By the time I clock out, I've made more progress than I have all week.

On my way home, I stop by the local flower shop.

The bell above the door jingles merrily as I enter, and the sweet scent of roses and lilies envelops me. Evelyn Winters, the owner, greets me with a knowing smile.

"Evening, Officer Michaels. What can I do for you today?"

I shuffle my feet, suddenly feeling like a teenager again. "I, uh, need some flowers. For a date."

Evelyn's eyes light up. "Oh, how wonderful! And would this date happen to be with a certain lovely librarian we all know?"

I can feel the heat rising in my cheeks. Sometimes I forget how fast news travels in a small town like Benton Falls. "Maybe," I mumble.

She laughs, a warm, grandmotherly sound. "Don't you worry. I know just the thing."

A few minutes later, I leave the shop with a beautiful bouquet of white roses and baby's breath. It's simple and elegant, just like Sadie.

At home, I spend an embarrassingly long time getting ready. I must try on every shirt I own before settling on a deep blue sweater that Sadie once said brought out my eyes. I check my reflection one last time, taking a deep breath to steady my nerves.

"You can do this, Michaels," I tell my reflection. "It's just Sadie. Your best friend. The woman you're in love with. No pressure."

That evening, I'm standing at the edge of the ice skating rink in the park, feeling like a kid at a middle school dance. The air is nippy, carrying the scent of fried goods and sweet treats from nearby food trucks. Festive lights twinkle all around, turning the park into a winter wonderland that would make even the Grinch's heart grow three sizes.

My heart races as I see Sadie approach, bundled up in a cozy scarf and mittens. She looks like she's stepped right out of a Christmas card, her cheeks rosy from the cold and her eyes sparkling with excitement.

"Hey, Ren!" she calls out, waving enthusiastically. "Ready to show off those smooth moves of yours?"

Everything feels normal between us, no lingering awkwardness from our moment in the library. Not sure if that's a good thing or not. But now's not the time for deliberation.

I chuckle, trying to ignore the butterflies in my stomach. "Oh, you know me, Sades. I'm as graceful as a newborn giraffe on ice."

She laughs, the sound like music to my ears. "Well, at least you'll provide some entertainment for the other skaters."

I present her with the bouquet, suddenly feeling shy. "These are for you."

Sadie's eyes widen in surprise, a soft smile spreading across her face. "Ren, they're beautiful. Thank you."

She buries her nose in the flowers, inhaling deeply, and I swear my heart skips a beat. When she looks up at me, her eyes are shining with an emotion I can't quite name.

We lace up our skates, our laughter mingling with the cheerful holiday music playing over the speakers. As we step onto the ice, I offer her my hand, hoping she can't feel how clammy it is through our gloves.

"Shall we, m'lady?" I ask, attempting a gallant bow that nearly sends me sprawling.

Sadie giggles, taking my hand, steadying me like always. "My hero," she teases, and we're off.

We glide hand in hand, our movements surprisingly synchronized. For a moment, everything feels perfect. The twinkling lights, the crisp winter air, Sadie's hand in mine—it's like a scene from one of those cheesy Christmas movies Sadie loves so much. I forget all my doubts, lost in the magic of the moment.

"Remember when we used to come here as kids?" Sadie asks, her voice filled with nostalgia.

I nod, grinning at the memory. "How could I forget? You were always showing off, doing those fancy spins while I clung to the wall for dear life."

She laughs, squeezing my hand. "Well, look at you now. A regular figure skater in the making."

As we round a corner, Sadie suddenly trips on what I can only assume is an invisible ice gremlin. My cop instincts kick in, and I catch her just in time, pulling her close to steady her. Suddenly, we're face to face, inches apart, and I swear I can hear my heart pounding louder than a perp banging on the interrogation room table.

The world seems to stop as our eyes lock. I can see

every fleck of gold in Sadie's hazel eyes, feel the warmth of her breath on my lips. For a split second, I think we might kiss. I lean in slightly, my brain screaming, *Now's your chance, Michaels! Don't blow it!*

But then, like a rookie freezing up during his first arrest, I pull back. Uncertainty and nerves get the better of me, and the moment slips away.

We both laugh awkwardly, the spell broken but not forgotten. "My hero," Sadie says again, but this time there's a softness in her voice that makes my heart do a triple axel.

As we continue skating together under the twinkling lights, I can't shake the feeling that something between us has changed. It's like we've crossed some invisible line, and there's no going back. And I might be okay with that.

We skate until our cheeks are rosy and our noses are numb, trading stories and terrible ice puns. "Hey Sadie, what do you call a bear with no teeth? A gummy bear!"

Sadie groans, playfully shoving me. "That was terrible, Ren. You should be arrested for that joke."

I grin, waggling my eyebrows. "Well, Officer, I'm afraid you'll have to catch me first!"

I take off across the ice, Sadie hot on my heels. We weave between other skaters, laughing like kids. When she finally catches up to me, we're both breathless and giddy.

As we finally make our way off the ice, I feel a surge of hope stronger than any cup of station coffee. Maybe, just maybe, this is the start of something amazing. And as

I watch Sadie laugh at another one of my terrible jokes, her eyes sparkling in the moonlight, I make a silent promise to myself. No more retreating. No more hiding behind the badge of friendship. It's time to lay all my cards on the table and hope that Sadie's willing to take a chance on us.

We stop at a nearby food truck, ordering hot chocolates to warm us up. As we sip our drinks, a comfortable silence falls between us. Sadie looks lost in thought, and I can't help but wonder what's going through her mind.

"Penny for your thoughts?" I ask softly.

She looks up at me, a small smile playing on her lips. "I was just thinking about how nice this is. Us here, like this. It feels... right, you know?"

My heart soars at her words. "Yeah," I agree, my voice husky with emotion. "It does."

As we say goodnight, Sadie gives me a quick hug that lingers just a second longer than usual. "Thanks for tonight, Ren," she says softly. "It was perfect."

I watch her go, my heart fuller than Santa's sleigh on Christmas Eve.

Tomorrow, I decide.

Tomorrow, I'll tell her everything.

Eight

ARTHUR

I appear at the bustling Christmas market, nearly bumping into a kid with a sticky candy cane. Great. Just what I need—to start my evening as a human lollipop. At least the kid didn't ask me if I was Santa Claus. Nothing against Santa, but if you live where I do and know of Saint Nicholas, you'd take the role of playing Santa very seriously and besides the beard, there are certain prerequisites—annoyed by little people isn't one of them.

The air is thick with the aroma of roasting chestnuts and apple cider. It stirs up memories I thought I'd left behind with my mortal coil. *Bah. Focus, Arthur. You're here on an assignment, not a trip down memory lane.*

I scan the crowd, searching for Sadie. There she is, admiring some overpriced ornaments like they're made of solid gold. Her hair catches the glow of the twinkling lights, and I swear I can feel the joy radiating off her from here. It's enough to give an angel cavities.

As I make my way towards her, weaving through the throng of merry shoppers—*and seriously, do humans always have to travel in packs?* — I spot Ren approaching from the opposite direction. He's dressed in jeans and a worn leather jacket, looking like he just stepped out of one of those TV cop shows.

"Hey, Sades," Ren calls out, his smile not quite reaching his eyes. "Found anything good yet?"

Sadie's face lights up. "Ren, you made it. Oh, you have to see these ornaments. Look at this little reindeer, isn't it adorable?"

I roll my eyes. Adorable. Right. More like a waste of good tree space. But watching Ren's face soften as Sadie chatters on, I can't help but feel a twinge of... something. Not that I'm going soft or anything. It's probably just indigestion from all this sickeningly sweet holiday cheer.

Just as I'm about to interrupt their little ornament love fest, a gust of wind carries a familiar voice across the market. "Well, well, if it isn't Benton Falls' finest librarian and her loyal protector!"

Oh, for the love of all that's holy. Ethan. Mr. Perfect Hair himself, strutting up like he owns the place. I watch Sadie's cheeks flush, and I can practically hear Ren's teeth grinding from here. He is not making my job any easier. I really want to dislike the guy, but my angel intuition tells me he's far from the naughty list.

"Ethan." Sadie exclaims. "I didn't know you'd be here tonight."

"And miss the chance to see you? Never," Ethan

replies with a wink that would make even Cupid roll his eyes.

I feel a growl building in my throat. This is getting us nowhere fast. Time for a little divine intervention, Arthur style.

With a thought, I summon a gust of wind. It whips around Ren and Sadie, tangling their scarves together. Ha! Let's see Mr. Perfect Hair compete with that.

"Oh!" Sadie gasps, stumbling slightly.

Ren's arms are around her in an instant. "I've got you, Sades. Here, let me help with that knot."

Their fingers brush as they work to untangle themselves, and I don't miss the spark that passes between them. That's more like it. Maybe there's hope for these two yet.

"Thanks, Ren," Sadie says softly, her eyes meeting his for a long moment.

Ethan clears his throat. "So, shall we explore the market? I hear there's a booth selling the most exquisite handcrafted bookmarks."

I snort. Bookmarks. Really? That's his big move?

As they meander between the stalls, I trail behind, my mind working overtime. This is going to be harder than I thought. How am I supposed to help these two see what's right in front of them when they're both as blind as bats?

I glance up at the starry sky, half expecting to see Henry's knowing smirk. "You could give me a little help here, you know," I mutter under my breath. But of course, there's no response. Just me fumbling through this assignment like a cat among cherubs.

Well, if subtle won't cut it, maybe it's time to be a bit more... direct. I square my shoulders and pick up my pace. Time to show these humans what a real guardian angel can do. So what if I'm still in training.

As the market closes for the night, I watch Ethan and Ren say their goodbyes to Sadie. Ethan, the smooth operator, presses a kiss to Sadie's hand like he's auditioning for a period drama. Ren, on the other hand, goes in for a bear hug that looks about as comfortable as squeezing a cactus.

I shake my head. "Amateurs," I mutter under my breath. I don't have time for this. Christmas Eve is on its way.

Before I can stop myself, I'm sidling up to Sadie as she admires a display of handmade scarves. "You know," I say, trying to channel some of that grandfatherly wisdom Henry's always going on about, "sometimes the best gifts are the ones we already have. Don't be so quick to toss aside what you and Ren share. His feelings for you run deeper than that pretty boy's ever could."

Sadie's brow furrows, like I've just asked her to solve a complex math problem. She fiddles with one of those friendship bracelets on her wrist—probably another one of Ren's awkward attempts at showing affection.

"I... I don't know what you mean," she stammers. "Ren and I are just friends."

I resist the urge to roll my eyes, knowing she's not as

dense as a fruitcake and smile. I search her eyes and see the answer I've always known shining back at me.

All I have to do is make her see it, too.

"Yes, you and Ren have one of the truest friendships I've ever seen."

Sadie's brow furrows and I can almost see Ren's face pictured in her mind.

"But have you ever considered your friendship with Ren is only the beginning?" I turn on my heel, leaving her something to ponder.

I've planted the seed. Now let's see if she allows it to grow.

In my celestial garden, the eternal sunshine hits me like a spotlight, and I squint against its cheery brightness—in heaven, there's no escaping the relentless cheer. I want to be optimistic about my progress with Sadie tonight, but I'm not sure.

I make my way to a scraggly bur oak that's been giving me more trouble than Ren and Sadie combined. As I prune its unruly branches, I can't help but draw parallels.

"You're just like those two, aren't you?" I grumble at the tree. "Stubborn, set in your ways, refusing to grow in the right direction, no matter how much I try to guide you."

The tree, unsurprisingly, doesn't respond. But as I work, I hum an old Christmas carol. Something about peace on earth and goodwill towards men. Huh. Maybe this assignment is rubbing off on me more than I'd like to admit.

I step back to admire my handiwork on the oak. It's looking better, I have to admit. Maybe there's hope for it yet. Just like there might be hope for Ren and Sadie.

"Well, well," a familiar voice says behind me. "Look who's gone soft."

I turn to see Henry, his eyes twinkling with their usual mix of mischief and know-it-all wisdom.

"I haven't gone soft," I grumble. "I'm just... adapting to the assignment."

Henry chuckles, the sound grating on my nerves like sleigh bells after a long night of caroling. "Sure, Arthur. Whatever you say."

I wipe my brow, more out of habit than necessity. "I just wish I could sprinkle some sense into Sadie. Ren's feelings are as obvious as Rudolph's nose, but she might as well be blindfolded."

"Patience, old friend," Henry says, clapping me on the shoulder. "Love, like your gardens, needs time to grow. You've planted the seeds. Now you've got to let them do their thing."

I furrow my brow. That was my line. What's Henry doing in my head? I grunt in response, knowing we're both right. But patience with plants is one thing — something I have and can give—patience with humans is a whole other garden, one I know nothing about tending.

Before I ponder this too long, Henry wanders off,

probably after the next angel in training. I turn back to my garden. The oak stands tall and proud, its branches reaching towards the heavens with new vigor.

"Alright," I mutter to myself. "If this stubborn old tree can shape up, maybe there's hope for those two lovebirds yet."

As I feel the pull of materialization, I take one last look at my celestial garden. "Don't you dare slack off while I'm gone," I warn the plants sternly. But there's a softness in my voice that wasn't there before.

Maybe, just maybe, I'm starting to understand this whole friendship and love business after all. But don't quote me on that. I've still got a reputation to maintain.

Nine

ARTHUR

T he warm-up scales of young musicians fill the air as I walk into the high school auditorium for the annual Christmas concert—apparently a hot spot for a December Friday night in Benton Falls. The cacophony of instruments tuning reminds me of the celestial choir practice, though with considerably less harmony. I smile to myself, remembering the last time Gabriel hit a particularly high note and shattered a few halos.

I scan the crowd, my angelic senses picking up on the swirling emotions filling the space. There's excitement, nervousness, and... ah, there it is. The complicated tangle of feelings I've come to associate with Ren and Sadie. Speaking of which...

I spot Sadie and her friend chatting animatedly near the entrance, and I make my way over, trying to look as casual as a man with a full white beard can at a Christmas musical. Laughter frolics through the air, mingling with the excitement of the crowd.

"Arthur!" Sadie calls out, waving me over. Her smile is warm and genuine, and I feel a little tug in my chest. These humans are growing on me, though I'd never admit it out loud. It's not exactly part of the guardian angel handbook to get attached.

"Evening, Sadie," I reply, my voice gruff but not unkind. "Quite a turnout tonight."

Sadie beams, gesturing to her friend. "Arthur, I'd like you to meet Gabby. She's the high school orchestra teacher. Gabby, this is Arthur, our new library volunteer."

Gabby extends her hand, her auburn curls bouncing as she moves. "It's so nice to meet you, Arthur. Sadie's told me what a help you've been to her."

I shake her hand, fighting back a smile. "Being a library volunteer is great. It's the only place I get to tell people 'shhh' all day and actually get thanked for it," I joke, surprising myself with the ease of the banter.

As we chat, I notice Ren approaching, his starched police uniform a stark contrast to the festive decorations. He offers Sadie a warm hug, and I don't miss the way his eyes light up when she smiles at him. It's like watching a flower turn towards the sun, and I feel a surge of hope for my assignment.

But then I detect the slightest tensing of Ren's shoulders as Ethan strolls over, greeting everyone with his usual charm. Ah, the plot thickens, as they say in those human novels.

"Sadie, you look stunning tonight," Ethan says, his

ERICA PENROD

eyes twinkling. "That sweater really brings out the green in your eyes."

I watch as Ren's jaw tightens almost imperceptibly. If I didn't have angelic perception, I might have missed it. "Hey, Ethan," he says, his voice forcedly casual. "Didn't know you were into classical music."

Ethan shrugs, flashing a disarming smile. "I'm a man of many interests. Plus, how could I miss Sadie's favorite event of the year?"

I resist the urge to roll my eyes and how does Ethan know that, anyway? He only met Sadie a handful of days ago. Humans and their mating rituals are more complicated than navigating the celestial bureaucracy.

The concert begins, and I genuinely enjoy the music, despite the occasional sour note. It's not quite up to heavenly choir standards, but there's a charm to the earnest efforts of these young musicians. I notice Ren and Sadie's fingers brush occasionally on the armrest. The electricity flowing between them is enough to power the hotline to heaven. I make a mental note to request a blessing for their budding relationship.

Throughout the show, Sadie's gaze drifts between Ren and Ethan. She seems conflicted, and I feel a surge of protectiveness. I may be here on a mission, but I can't help caring about these people. It's a strange feeling, this emotional investment. Is this what Henry meant when he said this assignment would change me?

At intermission, Ethan maneuvers Sadie under the mistletoe. I watch as he launches into what sounds like a heartfelt speech about his feelings for her. This wasn't on my agenda for the evening. I briefly consider using my divine strength to "accidentally" knock over the mistletoe, but quickly dismiss the idea. No messing with free will, after all.

"Sadie, I know we haven't known each other long, but I feel a connection with you I can't ignore," Ethan says, his voice low and earnest. "You're not just beautiful, you're kind, intelligent, and passionate about what you do. I..." He falters as though he wants to say more but falls on, "I would love to take you out and see where this goes."

Sadie listens politely, but I notice her fingers toying with the friendship bracelet Ren gave her. "Ethan, I... I'm flattered, really. But I..."

Ren, poor guy, is trying his best to look unaffected, but I can see the hurt in his eyes as he disappears into the crowd. I wish I could tell him it's going to be okay, but that's not how this works. Sometimes, I think, the hardest part of being a guardian angel is knowing when to step back and let things unfold naturally.

As Ethan finishes his declaration, Sadie retreats to the lobby, looking overwhelmed. I follow, concerned. Gabby breaks free from the crowd of congratulating parents and joins us, offering a supportive squeeze of Sadie's arm.

"You okay, kiddo?" I ask, my heart swelling with empathy in the face of Sadie's distress. "I saw you talking to Ethan." I offer a sympathetic smile. "He seemed a little... intense."

Sadie sighs, leaning against the wall, next to a life size

nutcracker. "Ethan's great," she confesses. "He's charming and we have so much in common. But..."

"But?" Gabby prompts gently.

Sadie fiddles with her bracelet again. "But I'm not sure I feel that way about him, plus—there's Ren," she says with a sigh.

Gabby grins as though Sadie's declaration isn't news.

But it is to me—or at least a confirmation. I feel a warmth spread through me at her words. This is what I've been hoping to hear. Given my human experience, I didn't dare believe I'd interpreted Sadie's feelings for Ren correctly. I'd hoped, I'd prayed, but now, I knew I was right, knew she—

Suddenly, chaos erupts. Someone knocks over the nutcracker from the other side. The statue topples over, striking Sadie. She crumples to the ground as Gabby cries out in horror.

Time seems to slow down as I watch Sadie fall. I reach out instinctively, forgetting for a moment that I can't interfere directly. My hand passes through her, useless, and I feel a surge of frustration and fear.

"Sadie!" Ren's voice cuts through the chaos. He's there in an instant, cradling Sadie protectively. "Someone call an ambulance!"

His fear is palpable as he tends to her. "Sadie, can you hear me? Stay with me, okay? Help is on the way."

As the EMTs arrive and whisk Sadie away, I stand back, watching the scene unfold. I feel a lump in my throat that has nothing to do with my assignment and everything to do with the genuine concern I feel for these people.

Gabby turns to me, her eyes wide with worry. "She'll be okay, right?" she asks, her voice trembling.

I put a comforting hand on her shoulder, surprising myself with the gesture. "She's in good hands," I assure her, my voice gentler than I've ever heard it. "And she's got all of us looking out for her."

As I watch Ren rush after the ambulance, his face a mask of concern and determination, I feel a mix of emotions I'm not sure how to handle. A profound angst cages me as anxiety over Sadie floods my being.

I glance upward, half-expecting to see Henry's knowing smirk. "Alright, alright," I mutter under my breath. "I'm worried. Happy now?"

I close my eyes and bow my head in prayer. "Please God, let Sadie be okay."

Was I supposed to have used my Miracle Card? *Dag nab it*, I wish I'd paid more attention to the instructions. What if there was something I could've done and didn't? Tears well in my eyes, and I'm surprised by the intensity of this human experience. I feel a swell of emotions in my chest and disappointment that I hadn't seen the accident coming. What good is a guardian angel if I can't even protect one beautiful soul?

As the night draws to a close, I'm left with more questions than answers. Should I got to the hospital? Stay out of the way? I decide to return to the celestial realm for guidance. With a thought, I transport myself to the heavenly gardens, my sanctuary among the stars. The memorable scent of jasmine and stardust fills my senses, a stark contrast to the pine and cinnamon of the earthly Christmas concert.

Intending to find Henry, I start towards the Angel Institute as I hear a familiar voice call out. "Troubled, Arthur?"

I turn to see Henry approaching, his silver hair gleaming in the soft light of the eternal day. "Henry," I greet him, my voice heavy with the weight of my thoughts. "I... I don't know if I'm cut out for this. I couldn't protect Sadie. I couldn't stop her from getting hurt."

Henry's eyes soften with understanding. "Ah, but that's not your job, my friend. You're there to guide, not to shield. Sometimes, the greatest growth comes from facing challenges."

I sigh, running a hand through my beard. "But will she be okay? I'm worried Henry, I care about them. Sadie, Ren... even Ethan. I want them to be happy."

"And that, Arthur," Henry says, placing a comforting hand on my shoulder, "is why you're perfect for this job. Your capacity for love and empathy is what will help them most."

No one has ever described me like that. As Henry's words sink in, I feel a renewed sense of purpose stirring within me. Maybe I can't protect them from every harm, but I can be there to support them, to guide them towards the love and happiness they deserve.

With a deep breath, I'm ready to go back. There's still work to be done.

"Thank you, Henry," I say, feeling more centered than I have in days.

Henry nods, a knowing twinkle in his eye. "Go on then. Your humans need you."

And with that, I feel the recognizable pull of Earth calling me back. As I materialize in Benton Falls once more, I silently vow to do whatever it takes to help Ren and Sadie find their way to each other. After all, isn't that what Christmas miracles are all about?

Ten

REN

I'm lying in an uncomfortable chair in Sadie's hospital room, my body aching from the tension of the past few hours. The sterile smell of antiseptic mixes with the faint scent of Sadie's vanilla perfume, creating a bizarre cocktail that makes my stomach churn. My mind keeps replaying the events of the concert earlier tonight, like a broken record stuck on the worst possible track.

One minute, we were all enjoying the soaring music and thunderous applause. The next, during intermission outside the auditorium, Ethan was telling Sadie how he feels, and I was making my getaway—until I heard a sickening crash. I ran towards the sound to find a giant nutcracker prop toppled over, with someone lying beneath it—not someone—Sadie.

My heart split in two as I rushed to her. Decades of friendship flashed before my eyes. The weight of my responsibility to protect her bears down on me, and I can't breathe.

I've let her down.

I've always been Sadie's protector. That's my job. When Carrie Mull shoved Sadie on the playground in the third grade, Carrie Mull got a handwritten warning that if she ever touched Sadie again, she'd never find her library book and neither would scary Mrs. Walters, the school librarian. And she's done the same for me.

Just like she was for me when my parents' marriage came undone. She was the unshakable force that reminded me love could endure, even when everything else was falling apart. She's always been there for me— and my stupid pride had me running away.

I don't care if she wants to date Ethan, I just need her to be okay.

Now, I feel that same fierce protectiveness coursing through me as I sit by her side, waiting for her to wake up.

The harsh fluorescent lights of the hospital flicker overhead, casting an eerie glow that makes Sadie look even paler than she is. My eyes never stray from her face, watching for any sign of movement. Her breathing is steady but shallow, and I lean closer, listening for every breath, as if my every happiness depends on it.

I hold her hand, my strong, calloused fingers feeling useless against her fragility. A tidal wave of memories rolls in, leaving a scattering of pictures across the sand. I see us in our prom photos, where I surprised her with a corsage made of her favorite daisies. I remember lazy summer days on her porch swing, as she dissected literary classics with the same intensity I'd used to crack a tough case.

A soft murmur escapes Sadie's lips, and my heart

leaps in my chest. I squeeze her hand gently, willing her to wake up, to give me any sign that she's okay. "Sadie, it's Ren. I'm right here," I whisper, my voice cracking.

Slowly, her eyes flutter open, and I feel a surge of relief wash over me. She looks disoriented at first, but then her gaze focuses on me, and I see a flicker of recognition, a hint of a smile playing on her lips.

"Ren," she says weakly, her voice barely more than a whisper. I lean in closer, my heart pounding like I'm in pursuit. "You're here."

"Of course, I'm here," I reply, my voice rough with emotion. "I'm not going anywhere, Sadie. You couldn't get rid of me if you tried. And believe me, you've tried, like the time you ditched me in the haunted house."

She smiles as her hand grips mine weakly, but the connection feels like a lifeline, grounding both of us in this moment.

"What happened?" Sadie asks, her brow furrowing in confusion.

I take a deep breath, trying to keep my voice steady. "There was an accident at the concert. During intermission, that giant nutcracker prop in the foyer toppled over. You were... you were hit."

Sadie's eyes widen slightly as the memory seems to come back to her. "Oh..." She seems to drift away for a moment. "I remember the crash. Everything after that is a blur."

"Yeah, well, you gave us all quite a scare," I say, attempting a smile that probably looks more like a grimace. "But you're okay now. The doctor says you have a mild concussion, and they want to keep you overnight for observation. Just to be safe."

Sadie nods slowly, wincing a little at the movement. "My head feels like it's been through the spin cycle."

"That's one way to put it," I chuckle softly. "Just take it easy, okay? No chasing down overdue library books for a while."

She smiles weakly at my attempt at humor, then her expression turns serious. "Ren, thank you for being here. I don't know what I'd do without you."

The sincerity in her words makes my heart swell with a fierce, protective love that's more powerful than any law in the books. "Hey, that's what friends are for, right? Gingerbread house construction, hot chocolate therapy, and concussion watch."

Sadie laughs softly, then winces again. "Ow. Don't make me laugh. It hurts."

"Sorry," I say, giving her hand a gentle squeeze. "I'll try to be less charming."

"Good luck with that," she murmurs, her eyes drooping.

"You should rest," I tell her, noticing her fatigue. "I'll be right here when you wake up."

Sadie's eyes flutter open again, a look of concern crossing her face. "Ren, you don't have to stay. It's late, and I'm sure you have work tomorrow."

I shake my head firmly. "I'm not going anywhere, Sades. Wild horses couldn't drag me away. Or wild reindeer, given the season."

"But—"

"No buts," I interrupt gently. "I'm staying. End of discussion."

A soft smile plays on her lips as she relaxes back into the pillows. "Okay," she whispers, her eyes closing. "Thank you, Ren."

As she drifts off to sleep, I settle back into the uncomfortable chair, my eyes never leaving her face. The steady beep of the heart monitor provides a soothing background rhythm, and I match my breathing to its steady pace.

In the hospital's quiet room, with Sadie's hand still in mine, I allow myself to really look at her. The soft curve of her cheek, the gentle flutter of her eyelashes, the way her chestnut hair fans out on the pillow... She's beautiful, and not for the first time, I feel my heart constrict with a longing that goes far beyond friendship.

I've spent years tamping down these feelings, convincing myself that our friendship was too precious to risk. But sitting here, watching her sleep, feeling the relief of knowing she's going to be okay... I can't help but wonder if I've been a fool all along.

The night wears on, and I drift between wakefulness and sleep, never fully letting my guard down. Each time I open my eyes, my gaze immediately goes to Sadie, checking that she's still breathing, still okay.

As the first light of dawn filters through the hospital blinds, I make a silent vow to myself. No more hiding, no more pretending. Life's too short, and Sadie means too much to me. When she's better, when the time is right, I'm going to tell her how I feel.

Because Sadie hasn't just been my best friend all these years. She's been the keeper of my heart, the one person who knows me better than I know myself. And maybe, just maybe, she feels the same way.

With that thought, I allow myself a small smile. Who knew it would take a falling nutcracker to knock some sense into me? As I watch the sunrise paint Sadie's sleeping face in soft golden hues, I feel a sense of peace settle over me.

Closing my eyes, I thank God for my blessings, for Sadie's recovery, and most of all, for allowing me to love a woman like her.

Eleven

REN

The evening chill nips at my face as I pull up to Sadie's apartment building, but my resolve to take care of her keeps me warmer than any jacket could. I balance a container of homemade chicken soup and a small bag of her favorite snacks in one arm while I ring the doorbell with the other. My heart does its usual Sadie-induced gymnastics as I wait, and I silently curse it for being so predictable.

The door swings open, and there she is. Sadie's smile is as bright as ever, despite the faint bruises from the accident that make my chest tighten with renewed concern. "Hey, Ren," she greets softly, her voice a balm to my frayed nerves.

"Hey, Sades," I reply, stepping inside. The acquainted warmth of her apartment wraps around me like a comforting blanket, chasing away the last of the winter chill. The scent of pine from her small Christmas tree mingles with the vanilla of her favorite candle, creating a uniquely Sadie aroma that I'd bottle if I could.

"You didn't have to do all this," she says, eyeing the soup and snacks with a mix of gratitude and exasperation.

I shrug, aiming for nonchalance but probably landing somewhere between "concerned friend" and "overprotective bodyguard." "Yeah, well, someone's gotta make sure you don't waste away on a diet of tea and old library books."

She rolls her eyes, but her smile widens. "My hero," she teases, and I pretend the warmth spreading through my chest is just from the temperature change.

After setting the soup on the stove to reheat, I help Sadie to the couch. She insists she's feeling better, but I can see the lingering fatigue in her eyes. I fluff the pillows behind her with the intensity of a bomb squad technician defusing a particularly tricky explosive.

"Ren, I'm not made of glass," Sadie protests as I tuck a cozy throw around her legs.

"I know," I reply, my voice gruffer than I intend. "Just... humor me, okay?"

She softens, reaching out to squeeze my hand. "Okay. Thank you."

With the soup steaming in bowls, we settle on the couch. Sadie leans into me, her head resting on my shoulder, and I wrap an arm around her, drawing her close. The contact is both soothing and intoxicating, and I wish I could freeze this moment and live in it forever.

We turn on a classic Christmas movie, the kind we've

watched together countless times. The flickering screen casts a warm glow in the dim room, and we lose ourselves in the familiar story. Our laughter mingles in the air as we recite lines along with the characters, our voices a perfect harmony born from years of friendship.

Between sips of soup and bites of buttery popcorn, we joke about the cheesy dialogue and predict the next scenes. "But that's what makes these movies so perfect," Sadie chimes in.

The movie is perfect but not because of the sappy script or expected outcome. I steal a glance at Sadie. It's because of the woman seated next to me.

Our conversation drifts to her plans for returning to work on Monday. "You sure you're ready?" I ask, concern lacing my voice.

She nods, determination shining in her eyes. "I'm sure. Besides, those books aren't going to shelve themselves."

"I don't know," I tease. "With all the weird stuff that happens in this town, self-shelving books wouldn't even make the top ten list of strange occurrences." I think about the flood of calls we've had at the police station about odd goings on this Christmas season. "Plus, you have Arthur."

As the movie progresses, I inch closer to Sadie, her warmth and presence stirring emotions I've kept buried deeper than a cold case file. Her laughter, her scent, everything about her is intoxicating. My heart races, and I struggle to resist the urge to kiss her, knowing she's still recovering. I'm pretty sure there's a law against kissing concussion patients, and if there isn't, there should be.

Just as I lean in to adjust the blanket around her—and maybe, just maybe, to work up the courage to say something more—the doorbell rings, shattering the intimate moment like a suspect through a plate-glass window.

I rise to answer it, my heart sinking as I see Ethan standing there, holding a beautifully wrapped blanket. He looks like he just stepped out of a Christmas catalog, all perfect hair and a winning smile. I resist the urge to check him for hidden elf assistance.

"Ethan," I greet, hoping my tone doesn't betray the mix of jealousy and admiration swirling in my chest. "Come on in."

Ethan steps inside, his usual charm and warmth filling the room. "I wanted to check in on you. See how you're feeling." He presents Sadie with the blanket, explaining it's to keep her extra warm during her recovery.

"Thank you, Ethan." Sadie's eyes light up with gratitude. "You really didn't need to do that."

"It's no trouble at all." Ethan grins. "My mom likes to knit in her spare time and sent me with enough blankets to gift all the citizens of Benton Falls."

Sadie grins as she runs her fingers along the cozy yarn of the red blanket. "Tell her thank you and it goes perfectly with my Christmas décor."

I can't help but admire Ethan's thoughtfulness, even

as it stings like a paper cut from one of Sadie's beloved books.

We all settle back onto the couch, Ethan on one side of Sadie, and me on the other. The conversation flows easily, and despite my jealousy, I can't deny that Ethan is genuinely a great guy. But he's not the right guy for Sadie —I feel it in my bones.

"So, Ethan," I say, trying to be the good guy, "how's the new bookstore coming along? You must be excited about the grand opening."

Ethan's face lights up. "It's going great. Thanks for asking. We're on track to open right after Christmas. I'm hoping it'll be a nice post-holiday treat for the town."

"That's wonderful," Sadie chimes in, her eyes sparkling with enthusiasm. "I can't wait to see it. Benton Falls has direly needed a good bookstore."

I nod in agreement, even as a twinge of jealousy pinches my heart. "Yeah, it'll be nice to have somewhere to browse besides the library. No offense, Sades."

Sadie elbows me playfully. "Watch it, Officer. I might have to revoke your library card privileges."

We all laugh, and for a moment, it feels like we're just three friends enjoying a cozy evening. Then Sadie turns to me, a mischievous glint in her eye.

"Oh, Ren, did I tell you? Ethan is actually Kylie Ramirez's second cousin. You know, her family owns Casa Ramirez?"

My eyebrows shoot up in surprise. "No kidding? I love that place. Best enchiladas in the state."

Ethan grins. "I will pass along the compliment.

Though I can't take any credit for the family's culinary skills. My talents lie more in the realm of books than burritos."

"So that's why you chose Benton Falls for your bookstore," I muse. "Family connections."

"Partly," Ethan admits. "But also because I fell in love with the town when I visited last Christmas. There's just something magical about this place, you know?"

I nod, understanding all too well. My eyes drift to Sadie, and I think to myself that the real magic of Benton Falls has less to do with the town and more to do with the people in it.

"Well, we're glad to have you here," Sadie says warmly. "And I, for one, can't wait to see what kind of reading events you'll host at the store. Maybe we could even collaborate on some library-bookstore joint programs?"

"That would be fantastic!" Ethan exclaims. "I'd love to pick your brain about what events work well in Benton Falls."

As they discuss potential book clubs and author signings, I find myself both impressed by their shared passion and a little out of my depth. I may love reading, but I can't match their encyclopedic knowledge of the publishing world.

"Just don't forget about us common folk when you're planning all these fancy literary events," I joke. "Some of us are more 'True Crime' than 'War and Peace', you know."

Sadie laughs, patting my arm. "Don't worry, Ren.

We'll make sure there's plenty of stuff for off-duty cops too. Maybe a 'Donuts and Detectives' book club?"

I roll my eyes, but I can't help grinning. "Hilarious, Sades. I'll have you know I haven't had a donut in at least... twelve hours."

The evening continues with more laughter and easy conversation. As Sadie grows more tired, I notice Ethan checking his watch.

"I should probably head out," he says, standing up. "Sadie, thanks for having me over. I hope you feel better soon."

"Thanks for coming, Ethan," Sadie replies with a warm smile. "And thanks again for the blanket. It's perfect."

I stand up too, knowing it's time for me to leave as well. "I'll walk you out," I tell Ethan.

As we say our goodbyes to Sadie, who looks ready to fall asleep right there on the couch, I can't help but feel a mix of emotions. Gratitude for this cozy evening, concern for Sadie's recovery, and a renewed determination to finally be honest about my feelings.

Ethan and I step out into the cold night, our breath visible in the frosty air. As we walk to our cars, Ethan turns to me, his expression curious.

"Ren, can I ask you something?" he says. "What's really going on between you and Sadie?"

My heart pounds in my chest, caught between truth and the unknown. I've faced countless interrogations, but none as daunting as this. As I prepare to answer, I realize that this moment could change everything. The truth hovers on the tip of my tongue, ready to break free after years of confinement.

I take a deep breath, the cold air sharp in my lungs. "Ethan," I begin, my voice steadier than I feel, "the truth is..."

Twelve

ARTHUR

I'm perched on a comfortable armchair in the Evergreen Library, watching Sadie as she bustles around the checkout counter. Outside, the first heavy snowstorm of the season is picking up strength, turning Benton Falls into a winter wonderland. The wind howls, rattling the large arched windows, but inside, the crackling fire in the grand fireplace keeps the chill at bay.

"Looks like we're in for quite a storm," I comment, breaking the comfortable silence.

Sadie looks up from her work, a distracted smile on her face. "Oh, yes. The weather report says it might be the biggest snowstorm we've had in years."

I can't help but smile and think about Rebecca, our heavenly forecaster, and how she'd love to report on a snowstorm. My gaze comes back to earth to find Sadie watching me peculiarly. "Yes, should be some storm."

I can sense the emotional tides shifting inside her, torn between exploring her feelings for Ren and the gravity of their lifelong friendship. It's like watching a delicate flower trying to bloom in uncertain weather.

"Everything alright, Sadie?" I ask, trying to keep my voice gentle. "You seem a bit... preoccupied."

She sighs, setting down the book she'd been cataloging. "Is it that obvious? I don't know, Arthur. I just feel... confused, I guess."

Before she can elaborate, the library doors burst open, bringing in a gust of frigid air and swirling snowflakes. Ethan strides in, his sandy hair dusted with snow, carrying a paper-wrapped package.

"Sadie!" he calls out, grinning from ear to ear. "I just got this in at the shop and knew you'd love it!"

Sadie's eyes light up as Ethan presents her with the package. She unwraps it carefully, revealing a beautiful leather-bound book.

"Oh, Ethan! It's a first edition of 'Pride and Prejudice'! This is incredible!" She runs her fingers over the embossed cover, her face glowing with excitement.

"I remembered you mentioning it was your favorite," Ethan says, his voice warm. "I thought it would be perfect for the library's collection."

I watch their interaction, noting the easy camaraderie between them. But I can't help noticing that while Sadie is clearly touched by the gesture, there's something missing in her reaction. A spark that I've seen when she's with Ren.

As if summoned by my thoughts, the library doors open again, and Ren stumbles in, breathless from battling the intensifying storm.

"Whew! It's really coming down out there," he says, stamping the snow from his boots. His eyes land on Sadie and Ethan, and I detect a flicker of jealousy in his cobalt gaze.

"Ren," Sadie exclaims, her whole demeanor changing. "What are you doing out in this weather?"

He shrugs, trying for nonchalance. "Just wanted to make sure you were okay. The storm's getting pretty bad."

"You all better stay put until it passes." Sadie's concern for everyone's well-being seems to override her earlier concerns.

The four of us settle into a comfortable rhythm as the hours pass. Ethan and Sadie discuss books, their conversation peppered with literary references that go over my head. Ren busies himself re-shelving books, but I notice his jaw clenching whenever Ethan makes Sadie laugh.

During a lull in the conversation, Ren sidles up to me. "Hey, Arthur," he says quietly. "Got a minute?"

We move to a secluded corner, and Ren takes a deep breath. "I told Ethan how I feel about Sadie," he confesses. "He said he respects my feelings, but... he cares about her, too. We decided it's up to Sadie, even if she doesn't know she's making a choice."

I nod, impressed by their maturity. "That's very noble of you both. But don't you think Sadie deserves to know how you feel?"

Ren's eyes dart to where Sadie is laughing at something Ethan said. "I wanted to tell her, but maybe I shouldn't. I don't want to ruin our friendship," he mumbles.

As the afternoon wears on, I can feel the tension building. Ethan is charming and attentive, while Ren is stoic and dependable. Sadie seems caught in the middle, unaware of the silent battle being waged for her affections.

"How about some hot chocolate?" Ethan suggests as the evening approaches. "I make a mean peppermint cocoa."

Before Sadie can respond, Ren clears his throat. "Actually, how about I whip up my grandma's famous hot chocolate recipe? For old time's sake?"

The meaningful look he gives Sadie doesn't escape my notice, nor does the way her breath catches slightly.

"That sounds wonderful, Ren," she says softly. "I've missed your grandma's cocoa. You know I keep the ingredients stocked."

As Ren prepares the drinks in the small kitchenette, Ethan leans closer to Sadie. "So, about the bookshop's opening night," he begins. "I'd love for you to be there. Maybe we could grab dinner beforehand?"

Sadie smiles, but it doesn't quite reach her eyes. "That sounds lovely, Ethan. I'll have to check my schedule."

I can see that Sadie genuinely likes Ethan, but it's clear where her heart truly lies. As I watch this drama unfold, I realize that sometimes love needs a little divine intervention.

With a deep breath, I reach into my pocket and pull

out my Miracle Card. It feels like hope in my hand. Now that Sadie has recovered from her accident and I'm not feeling guilty for not using it, I decide not to miss a chance to bring Sadie and Ren even closer.

As Ren returns with the steaming mugs of cocoa, I focus all my energy on the card. Suddenly, the library is plunged into darkness.

Sadie gasps, and I use my angelic senses to guide her stumbling steps straight into Ren's arms. The cocoa mugs clatter to the floor, forgotten.

"Sadie?" Ren's voice is soft, uncertain. "Are you okay?"

"I'm fine," she breathes, and I can hear her heart racing. "Just... startled."

In the pitch-black library, I can sense their close-ness, feel the electricity crackling between them. The storm rages outside, but in here, time seems to stand still.

"I can't see a thing," Ethan's voice comes from some-where to the left. "I'll try to find some candles."

As Ethan's footsteps fade, Ren and Sadie remain frozen in their embrace. I hold my breath, willing Ren to seize this moment.

"Sadie," he whispers, his voice thick with emotion. "I... there's something I need to tell you."

"What is it, Ren?" Sadie's voice is barely audible over the howling wind outside.

I can feel Ren's heart pounding as he struggles to find the right words. "You're my best friend," he begins. "You've been there for me through everything. When my parents split up, when I was struggling in the police academy... you've always been my rock."

Sadie's breath hitches. "You've been there for me too, Ren. Always."

"But it's more than that," Ren continues, his voice gaining strength.

Come on Ren, spit it out.

"Sadie, I feel... more." He draws in a breath. "I love you."

The silence that follows is deafening. I strain my angelic senses, trying to gauge Sadie's reaction. Her heart is racing, her emotions a swirling tempest.

"Ren, I..." Sadie starts, but Ren cuts her off.

"Wait, please. Let me finish," he pleads. "I know I'm risking everything by saying this, but I can't keep it inside anymore. Sadie, I'm in love with you. I have been for years. Every time I see you smile, every time you laugh at one of my terrible jokes, every time you're there for me... I fall in love all over again."

The confession hangs in the air, heavy with years of unspoken feelings. I hold my breath, waiting for Sadie's response.

But before she can speak, the lights flicker back to life. Sadie blinks, momentarily dazzled by the sudden brightness. Then, to my horror, she pulls away from Ren; her face a mask of confusion and... is that fear?

"I... I need some air," she stammers, and before anyone can stop her, she's darting out the door into the snowy night.

Ren stands there, his arms empty, looking like he's

just watched his entire world walk away. Ethan emerges from behind a bookshelf, a box of matches in his hand and a look of resigned understanding on his face.

And me? I'm left wondering if I've just made a colossal mistake. As I watch Ren struggle with whether to follow Sadie or give her space, I can't help but question my actions. Did I push too hard? Was this too much too soon for Sadie? But there isn't much time. December 24th will be here before I know it.

Once again, I feel truly lost. Maybe I don't have what it takes to be a guardian angel. The snow continues to fall outside, blanketing the world in white, and I long for the simplicity of my heavenly garden. But as I look at Ren's anguished face, I know I can't give up now. Somehow, I have to fix this.

I close my eyes, sending up a silent prayer. "Henry," I whisper, "I could really use some guidance right about now."

As if in answer, a warm feeling falls over me and suddenly, I know what I have to do next. It's time to have a heart-to-heart with Sadie, angel to human. I should've known that the path to love isn't always straight and narrow. Sometimes, it's as winding and unpredictable as a snowflake's journey to the ground.

With a deep breath, I prepare to forge ahead. Apparently, this assignment might require more than one Christmas miracle.

Thirteen

REN

I wake up groggy, my head pounding like a thousand little hammers in Santa's workshop. The world outside my window is coated in a thick, icy blanket—remnants of last night's snowstorm that trapped us all in the library. But it's not the weather that's making my stomach churn. No, it's the memory of what happened in that darkened room, the words that escaped my lips like fugitives I'd been holding back for years.

"I love you."

Those three words hang in the air, more intense than any winter chill. I groan and bury my face in my pillow, the scent of pine from my Christmas-themed detergent —Sadie's idea, of course — filling my nose. It's a smell that usually brings comfort, but today it just reminds me of her.

Dragging myself out of bed, I shuffle to the kitchen. The hardwood floors are cold under my bare feet, a shock to the system that does little to clear the fog in my brain. I pour a cup of coffee so strong it could probably strip paint and pad into the living room.

I sink into the sofa, cradling the steaming mug in my hands. The heat seeps into my palms, but it does nothing to warm the chill of uncertainty in my chest. Sadie's text from last night plays on a loop in my mind:

"Ren, I... I need some time to think. I'll call you soon, okay?"

Part of me feels a rush at having finally laid it all out there. The idea of turning our friendship into something deeper is thrilling, like standing on the edge of a cliff and getting ready to dive into the unknown. But another part of me recoils, fearing that my confession will blow up in my face like a poorly executed sting operation.

Restless, I set down my coffee and lean back on the sofa, closing my eyes. Instead of flipping through photo albums, I let my mind wander through the gallery of memories I've collected over the years with Sadie.

Images flash behind my eyelids, vivid and warm. I see Sadie at our high school dance, radiant in a blue dress that matched my tie. The memory is so clear I can almost smell her perfume, a mix of vanilla and something uniquely Sadie.

Another memory surfaces: our impromptu road trip after college graduation. I can hear our laughter echoing in the car as we made goofy faces passing the "Welcome to Kentucky" sign. The taste of gas station coffee and stale donuts lingers on my tongue, a reminder of our youthful adventures.

More scenes play out in my mind: late night cram sessions in the library. Sadie's forehead wrinkled in concentration as she explains a complex topic to me for the umpteenth time. Holiday celebrations at each other's houses, the warmth of her family's welcome making up for the chill in my own home. Quiet moments in the park, just sitting on a bench and watching the world go by, comfortable in our shared silence.

Each memory is a testament to our unshakable bond, a connection that's grown stronger with each passing year. I realize now that these aren't just random moments —- they're the building blocks of something deeper, something that's been there all along.

Suddenly, understanding slugs me in the chest. It's different with me and Sadie. It's not like starting from scratch with a stranger—this is Sadie. My Sadie. We have a solid foundation, something real to build on.

And then Arthur's gruff voice seems to echo in my mind: "Be patient with her, kid. Look how long it took you to get up the courage to face your feelings."

Man, I don't know where Arthur came from or how he found Benton Falls, but I'm glad he did. He's right. I need to trust Sadie, the smart, adorable woman who will find her way to me. I know she will.

Walking to the windowsill, I stare at the framed photos there. Sadie and me laughing at the county fair, covered in powdered sugar from the funnel cakes. Us building a lopsided snowman in her front yard, my police hat perched crookedly on its head. Every picture is proof of our bond, something that goes beyond labels or timing.

With a deep breath, I feel a wave of calm wash over me. It's like when a case finally breaks, all the pieces falling into place. I know who my soulmate is, who has loved me through everything.

Now, I just have to wait for her to realize it too. But that's okay. After all, stakeouts are part of the job, and I've always been good at waiting for the right moment to make my move—or rather, my next move.

I pick up my phone, tempted to call Sadie, to explain everything that's running through my mind. Because she's my go to my ride or die. But I resist. She asked for time, and I owe her that. Instead, I send a simple text:

"Take all the time you need. I'm not going anywhere. You're worth the wait."

Setting the phone down, I turn to look out the window. The world is still blanketed in white, but now it looks less like an obstacle and more like a clean slate. A fresh start.

I only hope Sadie sees it that way, too.

Fourteen

ARTHUR

Ten days until Christmas, nine days left to complete my assignment. The weight of this deadline settles on my shoulders like a heavy winter coat as I push open the grand oak doors of the Evergreen Library. To my surprise, I smile at the familiar scent of old books and cinnamon that greet me. It's a far cry from the celestial gardens I'm used to tending, but there's something comforting about this place. The books stand tall on their shelves, silent sentinels holding countless stories within their pages. If only my assignment was as straightforward as organizing these volumes.

I chuckle to myself, shaking my head. "Ren and Sadie seem to have minds of their own," I mutter under my breath. "Makes herding cats look easy." I never imagined bringing two people together, who love each other as much as Ren and Sadie do, would be so difficult.

As I round the corner towards the main desk, I'm surprised to see Sadie already there, nestled in her usual window seat. The morning light streams through the frosted glass, casting a soft glow around her that makes her look almost angelic. For a moment, I'm struck by the irony—here I am, an actual angel, and yet this human woman seems to radiate a warmth and light that rivals anything I've seen in the celestial realm.

But as I draw closer, I can sense the turmoil beneath her serene exterior. Her brow is furrowed slightly, and she's absentmindedly twirling a strand of her hair around her finger — a nervous habit I recognize.

"Good morning," she says, looking up at me with a wry smile. "How did you know I could use a friend? It's almost like you've got a sixth sense."

Her attempt at humor doesn't quite mask the seriousness in her eyes, and I feel a twinge in my chest. These humans and their complex emotions—they never cease to amaze me.

"Just lucky timing, I suppose," I reply, trying to keep my voice light. "Everything alright?"

Sadie sighs, closing the book she'd been pretending to read. "I don't know, Arthur. I just... I have a lot on my mind."

I nod, understanding all too well. The events of the past few days—Ren's confession, the snowstorm, the palpable tension between Ren, Sadie, and Ethan—it's enough to make anyone's head spin. And here I am, an angel tasked with guiding them through this emotional minefield. Sometimes I think cultivating the most delicate of celestial flowers would be easier than navigating human hearts.

"How about we take a stroll?" I suggest, motioning towards the door. "There's some stuff we need to chat about, and I've always found a bit of fresh air helps clear the mind."

Sadie glances around the empty library and nods gratefully, gathering her coat and scarf. As we step out into the crisp winter morning, I'm struck by the beauty of Benton Falls in the snow. The town square looks like something out of a holiday postcard—pristine snow blanketing the ground, twinkling lights strung between lampposts, and the majestic Christmas tree standing proudly in the center. The sky above is a clear winter blue, and I feel a bit more upbeat despite the challenges ahead.

"You know," I begin, my breath visible in the cold air, "back in my day, I used to find peace playing in the dirt. Plants have always been easier for me than people, but you're not so bad."

I wink at Sadie, who gives me a soft smile in return. As we walk, our footsteps crunching in the fresh snow, I can sense her relaxing a bit. It's a small victory, but I'll take it.

"Looks like Ren's confession has really stirred things up for you," I say gently, removing my hat to run a hand through my beard. "And I get it—sometimes emotions are like a pot of spaghetti; they just need to be untangled."

Sadie looks at me sharply. "Did he tell you?"

I pause, caught in a moment of angelic dilemma. I can't lie—it's against the rules — but I also don't want to admit I overheard their conversation. That seems rude, even by human standards. Instead, I decide to spin the question back to her.

"How about you tell me how you feel about Ren?" I suggest, hoping my celestial poker face holds up.

Sadie is quiet for a long moment, her gaze fixed on the snow-covered path ahead. When she finally speaks, her voice is soft but filled with a mix of emotions I can barely untangle.

"Ren's confession... it's stirred up feelings I haven't allowed myself to think about," she admits, her cheeks flushing pink in a way that has nothing to do with the cold. "I'm scared, Arthur. Terrified, actually. But yes, I care about Ren. More than a friend. I think... I think I always have."

My heart soars at her words, but I keep my expression neutral. "That's a big realization," I say carefully. "What do you plan to do about it?"

Sadie takes a deep breath, her exhale creating a small cloud in the frigid air. "I need to be honest with Ethan before I can pursue anything with Ren. He's a good man, and I don't want to play games with anyone's heart."

I give her a reassuring pat on the back, marveling at the warmth and strength I feel radiating from her. "Honesty is a good thing," I say with a smile. "I think that's why it's a commandment."

My little joke earns me a chuckle from Sadie, and I see a new determination in her eyes. She's clearly got a plan and is ready to tackle it. I'm relieved to see her so focused—maybe my job isn't so hard after all.

As we loop back towards the library, I'm left with a sense of accomplishment. Sadie's figured out her next steps, and while I'm here to back her up, she's the one who needs to sort things out with Ethan before she can dive into whatever comes next with Ren.

"You know," I say as we reach the library steps, "I'm proud of you, Sadie. Matters of the heart aren't easy, but you're handling this as though they were pages in one of your beloved books—with a gentle kindness."

Sadie looks at me, her eyes shining with unshed tears and gratitude. "Thank you, Arthur. I don't know what I'd do without you."

As she disappears into the library, I glance up at the clear blue sky, feeling a connection to the heavens above.

"Well, Henry," I murmur, "looks like your old student might just earn his wings after all."

With a lightness in my step that has nothing to do with my angelic nature, I follow Sadie into the library. There's still work to be done, hearts to guide, and all before the bells toll. But for the first time since I started this assignment, I feel like I'm truly making a difference.

Stepping back into the library, I reach for the cart of books to be shelved and I can't help but smile as I watch Sadie move about her day with a newfound purpose and how happy it makes me to see her smile. I realize that sometimes, the greatest miracles happen in the most unexpected places.

And to the most unexpected angel.

Fifteen

REN

It's been days since I last heard from Sadie, and the silence is driving me crazy. I told her to take as much time as she needed, but I didn't think it would take this long. Every passing hour feels like an eternity, and my mind can't help but oscillate between hope and despair.

Is her silence a good sign?

Or am I setting myself up for heartbreak?

Every time my phone buzzes, I practically lunge for it, my heart racing like reindeer through a snowy night. The disappointment when it's not her is almost physical, a dull ache in my chest that I can't shake. I've never been this wound up over anyone before, and it's throwing me off balance. Me, Ren Michaels, the steady, dependable cop of Benton Falls, reduced to a nervous wreck by a woman I've known my entire life.

Finally, after what feels like years but has only been a few days, a text comes through: "We'll talk after the church Christmas pageant." Relief floods over me like a warm shower after a long shift, but anxiety quickly follows, settling in my stomach like a lead weight. The pageant. Of course. It's our annual tradition, one we've shared since we were kids. But this year, everything feels different.

As I pull up to the church, the historic building at 125 Oak Street looks like something out of a dream. Garlands drape over the entrance, and a giant wreath hangs on the heavy wooden doors. It's beautiful, but all I can think about is what waits for me inside. I take a deep breath, inhaling the fresh winter air, before stepping inside. The scent of pine and frankincense hits me, a recurring comfort that does little to calm my nerves.

The interior is breathtaking, as always. High, vaulted ceilings with exposed wooden beams tower above me, and the warm glow of candlelight dances off the polished hardwood floors. The soft strains of "Silent Night" played on the antique organ fill the space, and for a moment, I'm transported back to all the Christmases past, standing here with Sadie, our voices joining in harmony.

I spot Arthur in his usual spot at the back, looking more like Santa Claus than ever in a red sweater. He gives me a knowing wink as I approach, and I wonder, not for the first time, if there's more to this old guy than meets the eye.

"Evening, Ren," he greets me, his voice gruff but warm. "Ready for your big performance?"

I chuckle nervously, my hand instinctively going to

the back of my neck. "As ready as I'll ever be, I guess. Have you seen Sadie?"

Arthur's eyes twinkle mischievously, reminding me of the suspect who knows more than they're letting on. "Oh, she's around. Probably getting ready to knock your socks off."

"What?" I ask, my heart rate picking up. Does Arthur know something I don't? Sometimes I swear this guy has a direct line to the Almighty with the way he seems to know everything.

He shrugs, a small smile playing on his lips. "Just that sometimes, the things we're looking for are right in front of us. We just need to open our eyes to see them."

Before I can respond to his cryptic comment, I spot Sadie across the room. My breath catches in my throat. She looks stunning in an emerald sweater dress, her hazel eyes shining brightly. She's laughing at something Ethan says, her head thrown back, exposing the graceful curve of her neck. My heart sinks a bit, settling somewhere around my shoes. Ethan. Of course he's here. Charming, successful Ethan with his perfect hair and his new bookstore.

"Go on," Arthur nudges me, pulling me out of my spiral of self-doubt. "The show's about to start, and you've got a nativity to narrate."

I nod, swallowing hard as I make my way to the stage. Each step feels like I'm walking through molasses, my legs heavy with anticipation and fear. Sadie sees me approaching and excuses herself from Ethan, meeting me halfway. My heart does a little flip in my chest at the sight of her smile.

"Hey," she says softly, her eyes meeting mine. "Ready to bring the Christmas story to life?"

"As long as you're by my side," I reply, surprised by my boldness. Where did that come from?

A faint blush colors her cheeks, and for a moment, I forget about Ethan, about my fears, about everything except the way Sadie is looking at me right now. It's a look I've seen a thousand times before, but tonight, it feels different. Charged with possibility.

The pageant starts, and Sadie and I take our places on stage. As we narrate, our easy banter and natural chemistry are on full display. It's like slipping into a favorite sweater —comfortable, familiar, but somehow exciting too.

"And so Joseph and Mary traveled to Bethlehem," I say, my voice carrying through the church. I've said these words a hundred times before, but tonight they feel weighted with meaning.

"But there was no room at the inn," Sadie continues, her eyes meeting mine with a warmth that makes my heart skip a beat. Are we still talking about Mary and Joseph, or is there a subtext here I'm missing?

Throughout the performance, I notice Sadie's eyes occasionally drifting to the wings, searching for Ethan. A knot forms in my stomach, but I try to focus on the script. I'm a cop, for crying out loud. I should be better at hiding my emotions than this.

When Ethan takes the stage as the innkeeper, I can't

help but feel a twinge of jealousy at his charisma and charm. He delivers his lines flawlessly, of course. Is there anything this guy can't do? But as the pageant progresses, I catch him watching Sadie and me closely. There's something in his gaze, a dawning realization that I can't quite place. It's like he's seeing us—really seeing us — for the first time.

By the time we reach the finale, something has shifted. Ethan's performance has softened, and there's a genuine warmth in his interactions with both Sadie and me. It's like he's letting go of something, and I realize the guy's even cooler than I thought.

As the last notes of "Silent Night" fade away and the applause thunders through the church, I find myself swept into a tight embrace with Sadie. "Ren," she says. Her arms are around my neck, and mine encircle her waist, pulling her close. I can smell the vanilla of her shampoo, feel the softness of her sweater against my cheek. It feels like coming home.

There are tears in her eyes, emotion swelling in my chest. There's something so pure and profound in this moment, something that goes beyond friendship or romance. It's a connection that feels almost spiritual, as if the magic of Christmas has woven itself around us.

"Ren," she whispers, her breath warm against my ear. "You were wonderful."

I pull back slightly, my hands still on her waist. "So were you, Sades. We make a pretty good team, don't we?"

She nods, her eyes shining with unshed tears. "We always have."

There's so much I want to say in this moment, so many feelings threatening to spill over. But before I can find the words, we're surrounded by well-wishers and congratulations. The moment is broken, but the feeling lingers, a warmth in my chest that not even the coldest winter night could chill.

As the crowd disperses, Sadie turns to me once more. "Can we talk? Outside maybe?"

My heart leaps into my throat. This is it. The moment I've been waiting for, dreading, hoping for. "Of course," I say, my voice steadier than I feel.

As we make our way to the church steps, I catch sight of Arthur. He's watching us with a smile that seems to hold all the wisdom of the ages. He gives me a subtle thumbs up, and I feel a surge of courage. Whatever happens next, I know I've got at least one person in my corner.

The cool night air hits us as we step outside, the stars twinkling above like a thousand tiny Christmas lights. I take a deep breath, the cold air filling my lungs, clearing my head. This is it, Michaels, I tell myself. No turning back now.

I look at Sadie, her face illuminated by the soft glow of the church lights. She's never looked more beautiful than she does in this moment, and I'm struck by how lucky I am to have her in my life, in whatever capacity she chooses.

"So," I say, my voice barely above a whisper. "You wanted to talk?"

Sadie nods, taking a deep breath of her own. "Ren,

I..."

And in that moment, as I stand there on the church steps with the woman I love, I realize that no matter what she says next, I'm the luckiest man in Benton Falls. Because I have Sadie in my life, and that's the greatest gift of all.

Sixteen

REN

The church doors creak open, and Sadie and I step out into the crisp night air. The churchyard is bathed in a soft glow from festive lights strung up in the trees, casting a magical ambiance over the snow-covered ground. The scent of pine and wood smoke mingles with a hint of the sugar cookies Mrs. Johnson was handing out after the pageant.

I stand under a large, decorated tree, trying not to fidget like an inexperienced teenager. My breath comes out in little puffs of steam, and I'm acutely aware of how loud my heart is pounding. Sadie's a few feet away, looking like she's working up the courage to defuse a bomb.

"So," I say, aiming for casual and probably missing by a mile, "nice night for a chat."

Sadie lets out a shaky laugh. "Yeah, because nothing says 'casual conversation' like standing in the freezing cold under a Christmas tree that looks like it mugged a Hallmark store."

I can't help but chuckle. Leave it to Sadie to break the tension with a quip. "Mugging aside, there's no crime in being overdressed for the holidays, trees included." I add.

She smiles, but then her expression turns serious. "Ren, I'm sorry it's taken me so long to respond to what you said at the library."

I nod, suddenly finding the snow-covered ground fascinating. "It's okay. I figured you needed time to process my incredibly smooth moves."

Sadie snorts. "Oh yes, it was smooth alright, confessing your feelings in a pitch-black library while tripping over a book cart."

"Hey, I stuck the landing," I protest, grinning despite my nerves.

Her smile fades a bit. "I needed to sort through my feelings. And... I needed to talk to Ethan first."

At the mention of Ethan's name, my stomach does a somersault that would make an Olympic gymnast jealous. I clench my fists inside my coat pockets, trying to keep my face neutral, but I probably look more like I'm constipated.

Sadie must notice because she quickly adds, "No, Ren, it's not what you think. I had to tell Ethan that I only see him as a friend. I wanted to be honest with him before... well, before this."

Relief washes over me, but uncertainty still lingers. "So," I say, my voice gruffer than usual, "what exactly is 'this'?"

Sadie steps closer, close enough that I can see the snowflakes caught in her eyelashes. "This," she says softly, "is me telling you that you're more than just a friend to me, Ren Michaels."

And then she kisses me. It's not the slow-motion, music-swelling kiss you see in movies. It's a little awkward at first—our noses bump, and I'm pretty sure I stepped on her foot. But then we find our rhythm, and suddenly everything clicks into place.

When we pull apart, we're both a little breathless. I can feel a goofy grin spreading across my face. "Wow," I say eloquently. "That was..."

"Yeah," Sadie agrees, her cheeks flushed. "It was."

We both laugh, the sound echoing in the quiet night. I take Sadie's hand and lead her to a nearby bench, brushing off the snow before we sit. The cold seeps through my pants, but I barely notice it. All I can focus on is the warmth of Sadie's hand in mine and the way her eyes sparkle in the moonlight.

"I can't believe it took us this long to figure it out," I say, shaking my head. "Some detective I am."

Sadie elbows me playfully. "Well, to be fair, you were looking for clues in all the wrong places. Like that time you thought I was into you because I brought you soup when you had the flu."

"Hey, that was grade-A chicken noodle soup," I protest. "If that's not love, I don't know what is."

She rolls her eyes, but she's smiling. "You're ridiculous."

"You love it," I say, and then pause, realizing the weight of those words.

Sadie's smile softens. "Yeah," she says quietly. "I do."

We sit in comfortable silence for a moment, watching our breath form little clouds in the cold air. The Christmas lights twinkle around us, and in the distance, I can hear the faint strains of off-key caroling. It's a perfect moment, one I want to bottle up and keep forever.

"You know," I say, breaking the silence, "I've imagined this moment so many times, but reality is so much better."

Sadie looks at me curiously. "Oh really? And how did your imaginary confessions go?"

I feel my cheeks heat, and it's not from the cold. "Well, in one version, I heroically saved you from a runaway Christmas tree, and you were so overcome with gratitude that you declared your undying love for me."

Sadie bursts out laughing. "A runaway Christmas tree? Seriously, Ren?"

I shrug, grinning. "Hey, it could happen. Those things are treacherous when not properly secured."

"Uh-huh," Sadie says, clearly unconvinced. "Sure, it could," she chuckles.

We fall into another comfortable silence, and I find myself marveling at how easy this is. It's still us, still Ren and Sadie, best friends since forever. But now there's something deeper, this feeling that makes everything more vibrant, more alive.

"Tell me about your talk with Ethan," I say, surprising myself with how calm I feel about it now.

"He was... incredibly understanding," Sadie says. "He thanked me for being honest with him and actually encouraged me to follow my heart."

I feel a newfound respect for Ethan wash over me. "Remind me to thank him," I say, only half-joking.

Sadie chuckles, the sound vibrating against my chest. "I think he'll be happy for us. He's a good guy, Ren. I hope you two can be friends."

"Yeah, me too," I say, realizing I mean it. The jealousy and insecurity I felt before seem silly now faced with this overwhelming love I feel for Sadie.

"You know," Sadie says thoughtfully, "I think Arthur had a hand in all this."

I raise an eyebrow. "Arthur? Our resident Santa Claus lookalike? How so?"

Sadie shrugs. "I don't know, exactly. But he always seemed to be around at the right moments, saying just the right things. It's like he was... guiding us, somehow."

I think back on all the times Arthur appeared with his cryptic advice and knowing smiles. "Huh. Maybe he's secretly a love guru or something."

"Or a guardian angel," Sadie jokes.

We both laugh at the absurdity of it, but there's a part of me that wonders. There's always been something a little... otherworldly about Arthur.

"So," I say eventually, pushing those thoughts aside, "what happens now? Do we need to update our Facebook statuses or something?"

Sadie laughs. "Ren, neither of us has used Facebook in years. But I guess we should probably tell our friends.

And by 'our friends,' I mean the entire town, because you know how Benton Falls is."

I groan. "Great. I can already hear Mrs. Henderson planning our wedding."

"Bold of you to assume she hasn't already booked the church," Sadie quips.

We both laugh, and I pull her closer, marveling at how natural it feels. "Well, whatever happens, at least we're in it together."

Sadie nods, resting her head on my shoulder. "Partners in crime-solving and life, huh?"

"You bet," I say, pressing a kiss to the top of her head. "Though maybe we should start with partners in not freezing to death on this bench. Hot chocolate at my place?"

"Thought you'd never ask," Sadie says, standing up and pulling me with her. "Race you to the cars?"

"Oh, you're on," I grin, already moving. "Loser has to tell Arthur the good news!"

As we dash across the snowy churchyard, laughing and slipping like kids, I feel lighter than I have in years.

As we reach our cars, both out of breath and grinning like fools, I catch sight of a familiar figure near the church doors. Arthur is standing there, a satisfied smile on his face. He gives me a thumbs up before disappearing back inside, and I can't help but laugh.

"What's so funny?" Sadie asks, looking confused.

I shake my head, still chuckling. "Nothing. Just thinking about how sometimes, the best gifts are the ones you never saw coming."

Sadie smiles, squeezing my hand. "Well, Officer Michaels, I'd say we both hit the jackpot this year."

We stood next to Sadie's car. She turns to me—our hands are still entwined—and so is my heart. "Yes, I'd say we did."

I lean over and kiss her. Her mouth tastes sweet, like mint and vanilla, and this time, there's no fumble. As she reaches up and puts her arms around my neck. I put my hands on her waist as my pulse races. This kiss is everything I've ever dreamed about and I can't believe it's finally happening. I can't believe this girl I've known and loved my whole life is finally mine.

This is going to be the best Christmas ever.

Seventeen

REN

I jolt awake, momentarily disoriented by the dimming light filtering through the windows of my living room. The last remnants of a pleasant dream involving Sadie and a mountain of Christmas cookies linger in my mind as I blink away the fog of sleep. Glancing at the clock on the mantle, I realize it's already late afternoon.

"Shoot," I mutter, rubbing my eyes. I hadn't meant to doze off after church, but the combination of a hearty post-service brunch at Molly's Diner and the cozy warmth of my fireplace had lulled me into an unexpected nap.

As I stretch, working out the kinks in my neck from my awkward position on the couch, a brisk rapping sounds at my door. I can't stifle the smile that immediately spreads across my face. There's only one person who would show up unannounced, yet entirely expected, on our annual baking day.

I make my way to the door, my bare feet padding

softly on the warm wooden floors. The house is filled with the lingering scent of pine from the Christmas tree in the corner, mixed with the faint aroma of the cinnamon candle Sadie had given me last week. "It'll make your place smell like Christmas threw up in here," she'd said with a wink. She wasn't wrong.

Sure enough, when I swing open the door, there stands Sadie, loaded down with grocery totes brimming with supplies. That adorable lopsided grin is stretching across her face, the one that never fails to make my heart do a little flip in my chest.

"Were you napping on Christmas cookie day?" she chuckles, her hazel eyes sparkling with mirth. She doesn't wait for an answer, just brushes past me into the kitchen, the scent of her vanilla perfume mingling with the cool winter air that follows her inside.

I watch as she upends the bags with a flourish, an avalanche of flour, sugar, butter, and an assortment of festive sprinkles cascading onto my kitchen counter. "I wasn't napping," I protest weakly, following her into the kitchen. "I was just... resting my eyes."

Sadie turns to me, one eyebrow raised in disbelief. "Uh-huh. And I'm the Easter Bunny." She reaches out and gently brushes something off my cheek. "You've got a couch pattern imprinted on your face, Officer Nap-a-lot."

I feel my cheeks heat, but I can't help the laugh that escapes me. This is what I love about Sadie—how easily she can tease me, how comfortable we are together. It's always been this way, even before we admitted our feelings for each other. But now, there's an added layer of warmth, a spark of something more that makes every interaction feel like Christmas morning.

"Alright, alright," I concede, moving to wash my hands at the sink. "You caught me. But in my defense, I picked up a couple extra shifts this week."

Sadie's expression softens, and she comes up behind me, wrapping her arms around my waist and resting her cheek against my back. The simple gesture sends a wave of contentment through me. "I know," she says softly. "You work too hard sometimes, Ren."

I dry my hands and turn in her embrace, looking down into those warm hazel eyes that I swear can see right into my soul. "I don't mind. A couple of the guys had Christmas dance recitals to attend and I'm happy to help put." I drop a quick kiss on the tip of her nose. "Plus, we've got to keep this town safe for Santa to make his appearance."

Sadie giggles, the sound like music to my ears. "My hero," she says dramatically, placing a hand over her heart. "Now, are you ready to be my baking hero, too? We've got a lot of cookies to make, mister."

And just like that, we slip into the familiar comfort and excitement of our long-standing tradition. It's something we've done every year since high school, this marathon baking session to create treats for the town's Christmas festival. But this year feels different, special in a way it never has before.

As we pull out mixing bowls and measuring cups, the easy rhythm of our friendship—now blossoming into something more—takes over. Sadie preheats the oven while I measure out flour for our first batch.

"Remember those disastrous gingerbread men we made in 6th grade?" she teases, hip-checking me playfully as she reaches for the sugar. "Frankenstein would have been jealous of those misshapen monsters!"

I laugh, the memory vivid in my mind. "Hey now, we were prodigies! Those weren't gingerbread men, they were avant-garde gingerbread abstract art."

"Is that what we're calling it now?" Sadie snorts, cracking eggs into a bowl with practiced ease.

"Absolutely," I nod solemnly. "In fact, I think they belong in a museum. 'Exhibit A: The Evolution of Ren and Sadie's Baking Skills'."

Sadie's laughter fills the kitchen, and I can't help but join in. As our chuckles subside, I reach into a drawer and pull out a dog-eared folder. "But just in case our artistic talents fail us this year, I brought backup."

Sadie's eyes light up as I open the folder, revealing a collection of time-tested recipes we've accumulated over the years. Each page is stained with flour and butter marks, notes scribbled in the margins in both our handwritings. It's a tangible record of our friendship, of all the Christmases we've spent together.

"Oh, Ren," Sadie breathes, running her fingers gently over the pages. "You kept these?" She sighs when she comes to the last page. "You've even got your Grandma Ellen's chocolate chip cookie recipe. I love this recipe."

I shrug, suddenly feeling self-conscious. "Of course I

ERICA PENROD

did. They're... they're important to me. You're important to me."

Sadie looks up at me, her eyes shining with emotion. For a moment, we just stand there, gazing at each other, the weight of years of friendship and newly acknowledged love hanging between us. Then, with a mischievous glint in her eye, Sadie reaches into the flour bag and flicks a handful at me.

"Sap," she accuses playfully, but I can hear the affection in her voice.

I gasp in mock outrage, looking down at my now flour-dusted shirt. "Oh, it is on, Jameson!"

What follows is nothing short of a flour war, with both of us ducking and weaving around the kitchen, lobbing handfuls of the white powder at each other. By the time we call a truce, we're both covered head to toe in flour, laughing so hard our sides hurt.

"We're a mess," Sadie giggles, trying unsuccessfully to brush the flour out of her hair.

I step closer to her, my heart full to bursting with love for this amazing woman. "Yeah," I agree softly, reaching out to cup her cheek. "But we're a mess together."

The kiss that follows is sweet and floury, and absolutely perfect.

When we finally break apart, both a little breathless, Sadie grins up at me. "As much as I'd love to continue this, Officer Michaels, we have cookies to bake."

I groan playfully. "Duty calls, I suppose. But don't think this is over, Miss Jameson. I'll have my revenge."

Sadie just winks at me and turns back to the counter, picking up where we left off with the cookie dough.

For the next few hours, we bake in well-choreographed tandem, moving around each other in the kitchen as if we've been doing this dance our whole lives. Which, in a way, I suppose we have. We make all our usual favorites—buttery spritz cookies that melt in your mouth, fudgy brownies with a hint of peppermint, intricately decorated sugar cookies that are almost too pretty to eat.

The mingled aromas filling the kitchen are intoxicating—warm vanilla, rich chocolate, spicy cinnamon. It smells like Christmas and home and love all rolled into one.

At one point, I'm kneading dough for another batch of gingerbread—hopefully more successful than our 6th-grade attempt—, when I find my gaze lingering on Sadie. She's carefully piping delicate snowflake designs onto some sugar cookies. Her brow furrowed in concentration as she chews on her lip.

"You're amazing, Sades," I murmur, my voice thick with admiration. "At everything you do."

Sadie looks up, a light blush coloring her cheeks. "Thanks," she says softly, her eyes meeting mine. "You're pretty amazing yourself."

I'm keenly aware of the depth of feeling I hold for her in this moment and know it's only the beginning—I'm so excited to see what the new year will bring.

We work in comfortable silence for a while after that, the only sounds the gentle Christmas music playing from my old radio and the occasional timer ding from the oven. It's peaceful and domestic in a way that makes my heart ache with happiness.

As the last batch of cookies comes out of the oven, I glance out the window to see that the sun has set, painting the sky in shades of purple and pink. An idea strikes me.

"Hey," I say, turning to Sadie, who's just finished boxing up the last of the cooled cookies. "What do you say we go for a little walk? Check out the neighborhood lights?"

Sadie's face lights up. "Ooh, yes! Just let me grab my coat."

While she bundles up, I quickly whip up two mugs of hot chocolate, adding a dollop of whipped cream and a sprinkle of cinnamon to each. When Sadie returns, looking adorable in her puffy winter coat and knit hat, I hand her a mug.

"Ooh, liquid warmth," she says appreciatively, inhaling the rich aroma. "You spoil me, Ren Michaels."

I grin, pulling on my coat. "That's the plan."

We step out into the cold evening air; the snow crunching beneath our boots. The neighborhood is a winter wonderland, every house adorned with twinkling lights and festive decorations. We stroll arm in arm, sipping our hot chocolate and admiring the displays.

"Oh, look at the Johnsons' house," Sadie exclaims, pointing to a house that looks like it could be visible from space with the sheer number of lights covering it. "I think they've outdone themselves this year."

I chuckle, remembering the good-natured competition between the Johnsons and their neighbors, the Petersons, that's been going on for years. "I don't know. The Petersons' light up reindeer are pretty impressive. I think Rudolph's nose actually blinks in time to music."

We continue our walk, exchanging observations about the decorations and reminiscing about Christmases' past. As we round the corner back onto my street, a comfortable silence falls between us.

"Do you ever think about the future?" I ask suddenly, my breath puffing out in little clouds. "About... us?"

I feel Sadie's steps falter slightly, and for a moment, I worry I've said too much too soon. But then she squeezes my arm gently.

"I do," she says softly. "More and more lately."

I stop walking and turn to face her, my heart pounding in my chest. "And... what do you see?"

Sadie looks up at me, her eyes shining in the glow of the streetlights. "I see... this," she gestures between us. "Us, together. Making memories, building traditions. I see movie nights and baking days and quiet mornings. I see a future where my best friend is also the love of my life."

My breath catches in my throat. "Sadie," I whisper, overwhelmed by the emotion in her words.

She reaches up, cupping my cheek with her gloved hand. "What do you see, Ren?"

I lean into her touch, closing my eyes for a moment. When I open them, I pour all the love I feel into my gaze. "I see a lifetime of making you smile. Of protecting you, supporting you, challenging you. I see us growing old together, surrounded by books and plants and maybe a dog or two. I see... everything I've ever wanted, Sadie. And it's all wrapped up in you."

Sadie's eyes well up with tears, but she's smiling so brightly it could outshine all the Christmas lights in the neighborhood. "I love you, Ren Michaels," she says, her voice full of wonder and joy.

"I love you too, Sadie Jameson," I reply, my heart soaring. "More than I ever thought possible."

As we lean in for a kiss, snowflakes begin to fall gently around us. It's a perfect moment, one I know I'll remember for the rest of my life. In this moment, making memories and building traditions with Sadie by my side feels cosmically right, like this is exactly where I'm meant to be.

When we finally break apart, both a little breathless and grinning like fools, I take Sadie's hand in mine. "Come on," I say, tugging her gently towards my house. "Let's go warm up. I think we have some cookies that need taste-testing."

Sadie laughs, the sound like music in the quiet night. "Always thinking with your stomach, Officer."

As we walk back to my house, hand in hand under the gently falling snow, the Christmas lights twinkle around us, a visual reminder of the magic of this season. But the real magic, I think, is in the way Sadie's hand fits perfectly in mine, in the love that's grown between us over years of friendship, in the promise of all the Christmases yet to come.

We reach my front porch, and I pause for a moment, just taking in the sight of Sadie, cheeks flushed from the cold, snowflakes caught in her eyelashes. She's the most beautiful thing I've ever seen.

"What?" she asks, noticing my stare.

I shake my head, smiling. "Nothing. Just... thank you."

Sadie tilts her head, confused. "For what?"

"For being you," I say simply.

Sadie's expression softens, and she leans in to press a gentle kiss to my lips. "That, I can do." She murmurs against my mouth.

As we step back into the warmth of my house, the scent of freshly baked cookies enveloping us, I'm struck by how right this feels. Sadie and me, together, building a life filled with love and laughter and the sweet traditions we've created over the years.

It's not just the magic of Christmas, I realize. It's the magic of us, of friendship blossoming into love, of two people who have always been there for each other, finally finding their way to where they were always meant to be.

And as Sadie tugs me towards the kitchen, already debating which cookies we should try first, I know that this is just the beginning of our greatest adventure yet. Whatever the future holds, we'll face it together, with a batch of cookies and a whole lot of love.

After all, that's what true friendship—and love—is all about.

Eighteen

ARTHUR

I sigh, stepping into my garden, as a sense of satisfaction washes over me, as palpable as the warmth of the eternal sun. *Well, Arthur,* I mutter to myself, *looks like you might just earn those wings after all.*

My garden is a riot of color and fragrance, a testament to the beauty of creation. Flowers of every hue imaginable bloom in perfect harmony, their petals as soft as clouds and twice as beautiful. Of course, everything seems a little brighter with my assignment practically complete, and a few days early, too.

I brush my fingers against the velvety petals of a nearby rose, and I can't help but smile, thinking about Ren and Sadie. They finally admitted their feelings for each other, after what felt like an eternity of dancing around the issue.

"About time, you two," I chuckle to myself, as I pull out my shears and carefully snip away a dead branch. "I was thinking I'd need another century to sort you out."

The flowers seem to wink at me in the soft celestial light, as if they know I've done good work—with them and my assignment. I might even write a gardening book about this—'From Roses to Romance: An Angel's Guide to Cultivating Love'.

As I settle into my gardening groove, losing myself in the rhythmic snip of my shears and the earthy scent of freshly turned soil, a familiar shimmer in the air catches my attention. I look up to see Henry before me, shimmering like a celestial disco ball. I'm thinking he's here to schedule my dissertation early. But Henry's next words send my thoughts screeching to a halt like a chariot with square wheels. "Your assignment isn't complete yet."

I stare at him, bewildered. "What do you mean, not complete? Ren and Sadie are together. They've admitted their feelings. They're practically picking out china patterns as we speak."

Henry shakes his head, his expression grave. "Something is going to happen that will change things," he says, his voice taking on that mysterious, all-knowing tone that never fails to leave me unsettled. "You need to be prepared."

I do not know what Henry is talking about. "What could possibly go wrong now?" I demand. "They're perfect together. They've overcome their fears, their doubts. What else could there be?"

But Henry, true to form, remains cryptic. "Just be vigilant, Arthur. Your work isn't done yet."

And with that, he vanishes in a shower of golden sparks, leaving me standing there with my pruning shears in one hand and a half-trimmed rosebush in front of me. So much for my peaceful garden time.

As the implications of Henry's words sink in, my mind races faster than a choir of cherubs after too much heavenly nectar. Did I miss something? Ren and Sadie seem perfect together. What on Earth (or Heaven) could mess this up?

I try to return to my gardening, hoping the traditional task will calm my frazzled nerves. The flowers don't judge; they just grow. Unlike humans, who seem intent on complicating everything.

As I work, I start second-guessing every interaction I've had with Ren and Sadie. Maybe I should hover around them, make sure they don't undo all my good efforts. The thought makes me groan out loud. More human drama. Just what I need.

"I signed up to be a gardener," I grumble to a nearby rosebush, wondering if the wings are really worth it. "Not a relationship counselor."

The roses, unsurprisingly, offer no advice. But their silent presence is comforting nonetheless.

As I trim the last rosebush, a thought occurs to me that makes me chuckle despite my worry. "Humans," I mutter to myself, "why can't they be as easy to manage as plants?"

The blooms sway gently in the celestial breeze, as if in agreement. But invested I am, whether I like it—in Ren and Sadie—although I'm not ready to admit it out loud.

With a sigh that could rustle the leaves of the Tree of Life, I set down my pruning shears. It looks like my work on Earth isn't done yet. I take one last look at my heavenly garden. The flowers seem to wave goodbye, their petals catching the eternal light in a dazzling display.

"Wish me luck," I tell them. "I have a feeling I'm going to need it."

And with that, I feel the familiar pull of Earth calling me back. As I prepare to return to Benton Falls once more, I can't help but wonder what new complications await me. But one thing's for sure—I'm not about to let all my hard work go to waste. Ren and Sadie's love story is far from over, and I intend to see it through to its happily ever after.

After all, isn't that what guardian angels are for?

Nineteen

ARTHUR

The winter air is chilly as I appear at the annual Benton Falls Community Christmas Parade, but as an angel, the cold is an afterthought. The streets are alive with twinkling lights, each lamppost and building adorned with sparkling decorations that rival the stars in the heavens. The festive atmosphere is palpable, a tangible energy that even I, a gruff old angel-in-training, can't help but be affected by.

I inhale deeply, savoring the mingled scents of pine, cinnamon, and the unmistakable aroma of roasting chestnuts from a nearby vendor. It's a far cry from the perfumed air of my heavenly garden, but there's something undeniably charming about these earthly fragrances. They speak of warmth, of togetherness, of the very essence of this human celebration called Christmas.

As I scan the crowd, my eyes searching for Ren and Sadie, I can't help but marvel at the sea of smiling faces around me. Families huddle together, their breath visible in the frosty air, eyes wide with wonder at the spectacle before them. Children bounce on their toes in excitement, their laughter a melody that harmonizes perfectly with the distant strains of "Jingle Bells" floating on the breeze.

I decide to take a stroll through the parade, immersing myself in the festivities before I locate my charges. The first float that catches my eye is a massive snow globe, complete with swirling "snow" and a miniature version of Benton Falls inside. The craftsmanship is impressive, and I chuckle at the tiny ice skaters circling a pond in the center.

"Now that's attention to detail," I mutter, stroking my beard appreciatively.

As I continue down the street, I'm greeted by the sweet voices of a children's choir. They're perched atop a float designed to look like a giant Christmas tree, their angelic voices rising in perfect harmony as they sing "Silent Night." For a moment, I'm transported back to the celestial realms, reminded of the heavenly choirs. But there's something uniquely touching about these young human voices, filled with innocence and joy.

"Not bad," I nod, allowing myself a small smile. "Not bad at all."

The parade continues, each float more elaborate than the last. There's a gingerbread house that actually wafts the scent of freshly baked cookies, a winter wonderland complete with "real" snow—which I suspect is just cleverly disguised soap suds—and even a tropical Christmas scene with palm trees decked in lights and flamingos wearing Santa hats.

I can't help but laugh at the last one. "Humans and their imagination," I muse. "Who would have thought to combine flamingos and Christmas?"

As I pass by a group of street vendors, the aroma of hot chocolate and roasted chestnuts becomes too tempting to resist. I know I don't strictly need earthly sustenance, but surely it can't hurt to indulge a little? After a moment's hesitation, I buy a steaming cup of cocoa and a bag of warm chestnuts.

The first sip of hot chocolate sends a wave of warmth through me, and I close my eyes in appreciation. "Heavenly," I murmur, then chuckle at my joke. The chestnuts are equally delightful, their earthy flavor a perfect complement to the sweet cocoa.

As I enjoy my treats, I continue to take in the sights and sounds of the parade. A marching band passes by, their brass instruments gleaming in the lamplight as they play a rousing rendition of "Deck the Halls." The music sets my foot tapping, and I hum along despite my usual gruff demeanor.

"Well, would you look at that," I say to myself. "Even old Arthur can get into the Christmas spirit."

I spot a group of children excitedly pointing at something, and I follow their gaze to see Santa Claus himself riding atop a magnificent sleigh float. His hearty "Ho ho ho!" booms over the crowd, and I can't help but shake my head in amusement.

"Amateur," I mutter good-naturedly. "But I suppose he has a certain charm."

As the parade winds down, I finally spot Ren and Sadie near the town square. With all the Christmas spirit in the air, I forgot to worry about my assignment until I saw them. They stand close together, their hands intertwined, faces glowing with a happiness that seems to radiate outward. The sight brings a smile to my face, a feeling of warmth spreading through my chest that has nothing to do with the hot chocolate.

"Well, would you look at that," I mutter to myself, stroking my beard thoughtfully. Everything seems to be going fine.

I watch as Ren playfully swipes a candy cane from Mrs. Claus, presenting it to Sadie with an exaggerated bow.

Maybe there's nothing to worry about.

"For you, my lady," I hear him say, his voice carrying a note of tenderness that makes even my old heart soften.

Sadie accepts it with a curtsy, her laughter ringing out like bells. "Why, thank you, kind sir," she replies, her eyes sparkling with mirth.

Their easy banter, the way they move in sync with each other, the stolen glances and gentle touches—it all speaks of a deep connection, a love that has blossomed from years of friendship. It's picture-perfect, almost too good to be true.

As I observe them, a sense of pride and accomplishment washes over me. Look at them, I think. So happy, so in love. They've overcome their fears, admitted their feelings, and are building a life together. What more could I possibly need to do?

I chuckle to myself, imagining the look on Henry's face when I report back on my resounding success. "See, Henry?" I mutter. "They're just fine. Right on track."

I watch as Ren and Sadie stop to admire the live nativity scene. The tableau before them is a serene one—costumed townspeople portraying the holy family, shepherds, and wise men, accompanied by real animals. The gentle bleating of sheep and soft cooing of doves add an air of authenticity to the scene. I watch as Sadie's expression softens, clearly moved by the display. Ren wraps an arm around her shoulders, pulling her close.

"It's beautiful, isn't it?" I hear Sadie murmur.

Ren nods, his eyes fixed not on the nativity scene, but on Sadie's face. "Yeah," he says softly. "Beautiful."

Ren and Sadie stand close together, their hands intertwined, faces glowing with happiness. I decide to approach them for a closer inspection. "Well, if it isn't the happy couple," I say, and appear beside them. "Enjoying the parade?"

Ren's eyes light up. "Arthur!" He looks around, a baffled expression on his face. "Where did you come from? We didn't expect to see you here. Isn't it wonderful?"

Sadie nods enthusiastically. "It's absolutely magical. The lights, the music, the whole atmosphere... I don't think I've ever seen Benton Falls look so beautiful."

I stroke my beard thoughtfully. "Indeed, it is quite a spectacle. Tell me, what's your favorite part so far?"

"Oh, that's tough," Ren muses. "The marching band was pretty great. But I think I loved the live nativity scene the most. It just felt so... authentic, you know?"

Sadie squeezes his hand. "I agree. There was something so peaceful about it. And did you see the animals? The little lamb was adorable!"

I chuckle. "Yes, I saw. Though I must say, I'm partial to the gingerbread house float myself. The smell of those cookies was heavenly."

"Speaking of heavenly," Sadie says with a grin, "you look quite festive yourself, Mr. Arthur. Very Santa-like."

I harrumph good-naturedly. "Now, now, let's not get carried away. I'm not *that* old."

They both laugh, and the sound warms my heart. As we continue to chat about the parade, I can't help but feel a sense of pride. These two have come so far, and their love for each other is clear in every glance, every touch.

I feel myself relaxing, a sense of contentment settling over me. Surely, I think, they're solid now. What could possibly come between them? They've overcome their fears, admitted their feelings, and are building a life together. My job here must be done.

Could Henry have made a mistake?

Was he thinking of another assignment?

As I stand there, contemplating how anything could go wrong now, with so much love and joy in the air, a sudden flash of light blinds me momentarily. I stumble, grabbing onto a nearby lamppost for support. The world around me fades away, replaced by a disorienting vision.

I see Ren and Sadie outside in a crowded area, possibly the Christmas market. Ren is pacing back and forth, his face a mask of anxiety. He's talking to Sadie. I can't hear what he's saying, but Sadie's face crumples in confusion and hurt.

I shudder at their expressions. I don't know what is going on, but it's serious.

Suddenly Ren storms off, leaving Sadie standing there, tears streaming down her face. The vision fades as quickly as it appeared, leaving me gasping and disoriented. The joyous parade scene comes rushing back, the contrast so stark it's almost painful.

"Arthur? Are you alright?" Sadie's concerned voice breaks through my daze.

I blink, focusing on their worried faces. "Yes, yes, I'm fine. Just got a bit overwhelmed by all the excitement, I suppose."

Ren looks skeptical. "Are you sure? You looked like you saw a ghost for a second there."

"Oh, nothing so dramatic," I assure them, trying to keep my voice light. "Just an old man getting caught up in the Christmas spirit. Now, why don't you two go enjoy the rest of the parade? I hear there's a float coming up that shoots out candy canes."

Their faces light up at this, and with a wave, they head off into the crowd. I watch them go, my heart heavy with the weight of what I've seen.

"Alright," I mutter to myself, squaring my shoulders. "Time to earn those wings, Arthur. Whatever's coming, we'll face it head-on."

As the last echoes of the parade fade away and the town settles into a peaceful winter's night, I find myself filled with a mix of anticipation and determination. Whatever comes next, I'll be ready. I've never let a plant die on my watch, and I'm not about to let Ren and Sadie's budding romance be the first.

I've got this. One way or another, I'll figure this out. I only wish I had one more miracle card in my back pocket.

Twenty

REN

The crisp December 23rd air fills my lungs as I step into the twinkling city park, just south of Benton Falls' town square. The annual winter festival is in full swing, transforming our usually tranquil park into a bustling Christmas market. The festive atmosphere is infectious, and I can't help but feel a surge of excitement.

"They've outdone themselves this year." I murmur to myself, taking in the rows of charming wooden stalls and the towering Christmas tree at the center of it all.

Cheerful carols pipe through speakers strategically placed around the park, their melodies mingling with the enticing aroma of roasting chestnuts and the jovial laughter of families milling about. It's the perfect setting for a night of holiday fun, and I grin from ear to ear as I take it all in.

My smile stretches even wider when I spot Sadie

sauntering over, her radiant grin making my heart flip-flop in my chest. She's beautifully bundled in a forest green sweater, with her chestnut hair peeking out from beneath a cream-colored knit cap.

"Fancy meeting you here," I deadpan, trying to play it cool despite the warmth spreading through me in her presence. I can't resist hip-checking her playfully. "Ready for some hot chocolate?"

"You know it," Sadie smiles, and I don't need any cocoa. I'm already warm from head to toe.

We're both grinning as we reach the hot chocolate stand. The elderly couple running the booth greets us with knowing smiles—we've been fixtures at their stand every winter festival for as long as I can remember.

We've barely claimed our mugs of steaming cocoa before Sadie launches into one of her ridiculous made-up stories, this one involving a rogue elf, a malfunctioning toy-making machine, and Santa's secret stash of protein bars.

"So there's Tinsel, right?" Sadie gesticulates wildly, nearly spilling her cocoa. "He's trying to fix the Toy-O-Matic 3000, but he's only making it worse. Sparks are flying, toys are shooting out like projectiles-"

"Let me guess," I interject, grinning. "That's when Santa walks in?"

"Exactly!" Sadie nods enthusiastically. "There's Big Red, protein bar halfway to his mouth, staring at the chaos. And you know what he says?"

I lean in, playing along. "What does he say?"

Sadie drops her voice comically low, doing her best Santa impression. "Ho ho... oh no."

I can't help it—I burst out laughing, nearly snorting hot chocolate through my nose. "Sadie!" I gasp between fits of laughter. "You're going to be the death of me, I swear."

She grins impishly, clearly pleased with herself. "What can I say? It's a gift."

When I manage to compose myself, we turn our attention to the sledding hill that's been set up at the edge of the park. Children of all ages zoom down the slope on colorful sleds and inner tubes, their shrieks of delight carried on the winter wind.

"Remember when that used to be us?" Sadie asks, a hint of nostalgia in her voice.

I nod, smiling at the memory. "Yeah, until you decided it would be a great idea to try and sled standing up."

Sadie winces. "In my defense, it looked really cool in my head."

"Sure did," I agree. "Right until you wiped out and took out half the kids on the hill with you."

"Hey!" Sadie elbows me playfully. "I thought we agreed never to speak of that again."

I hold up my hands in surrender. "My lips are sealed. Your reputation as the cool librarian remains intact."

We spend a few more minutes cheering on the sledders and laughing at their spectacular wipeouts before I turn to Sadie with a mischievous grin. "Ice skating next?"

Sadie shakes her head in fond exasperation. "You

know I can't say no to that face," she sighs dramatically, but the excitement in her eyes betrays her true feelings. "Let's go, hotshot. Show me what you've got."

We make our way to the makeshift ice rink, rent our skates and lace them up with practiced ease. I can't help but think about the last time we were here, and I hadn't told Sadie how I felt. Now we're a couple—and now I plan to add some kisses to my ice skating routine.

As soon as we step onto the ice, muscle memory kicks in, and I find my balance quickly. Sadie, on the other hand, immediately grasps the wall, her legs wobbling like a newborn fawn's, like we hadn't just done this a couple weeks ago.

"Having some trouble there, grace?" I tease, gliding by with what I hope is effortless athleticism.

"Oh, shut up," Sadie grumbles good-naturedly. "We can't all be Captain Coordination."

I circle back, offering her my hand. "Come on, I've got you. Trust me."

Sadie hesitates for a moment before taking my hand, her fingers warm despite the chill in the air. "If you let me fall, Ren Michaels, I swear I'll—"

"You'll what?" I challenge, pulling her gently away from the wall. "Throw a book at me?"

"Don't tempt me," Sadie warns, but she's smiling. "I've got excellent aim and access to some very heavy encyclopedias."

We spend the next hour twirling, racing, and inevitably falling in spectacular fashion. Each time one of us goes down, we drag the other with us, ending up in a tangle of limbs and laughter on the cold ice.

"Okay, okay," Sadie pants after our latest tumble. "I think I've had enough near-death experiences for one night."

I help her to her feet, steadying her with a hand on her waist. "Aw, come on. Where's your sense of adventure?"

"I left it back on solid ground, along with my dignity," Sadie retorts, but she's grinning.

I don't want to miss this chance to make one more memory with this woman, so I lean in, our breath swirling in the air around us. Sadie looks up at me, the twinkling lights reflecting in her eyes, her pink cheeks and red lips taunt me like a gift under the tree—the tag with my name on it. I press my lips to hers as heat ripples from my head to my toes. My heart pounds and my pulse quickens as I take the kiss further, then I stop—

A wide smile covers my face as I remember we're in the middle of the rink with spectators all around us.

"Good call, Officer Michaels." Sadie grins as she reaches for my hand. "Don't want to get arrested for PDA two days before Christmas."

"No, we don't." I squeeze her hand, amazed at how she knows me so well.

By the time we stumble off the rink, our cheeks are flushed, our sides ache from laughing, and I'm pretty sure I'll have some impressive bruises tomorrow. But the warmth in Sadie's eyes as she looks at me makes it all worth it.

During a breather, we mosey over to the petting zoo area that's been set up near the edge of the park. A small crowd has gathered, mostly young families with excited children. We join them, watching as enraptured kids stroke the velvety noses of patient reindeer and coo over fluffy bunnies.

An unmistakable softness blooms in Sadie's gaze as she observes the scene. She's always had a way with children. Her natural warmth and nurturing spirit drawing them to her like moths to a flame.

"You're such a natural with kids, Sadie," I murmur, unable to keep the admiration from my voice.

Her crooked smile in response makes my heart stutter in my chest. "Thanks, Ren," she says softly, a hint of wistfulness in her tone. "Maybe someday, right?"

I swallow hard, pushing down the surge of longing her words evoke. "Yeah," I manage. "Someday."

Her question should've freaked me out, but it didn't —and that kind of freaked me out. But everything is different with Sadie.

As night falls, casting long shadows across the snow-covered park, we meander hand-in-hand through the holiday market. The park is lined with charming wooden stalls, each one overflowing with handcrafted treasures and seasonal delights. Twinkling fairy lights are strung overhead, creating a magical canopy that bathes everything in a warm, golden glow.

"Oh, Ren, look!" Sadie tugs on my hand, pulling me towards a stall selling handmade ornaments. "Aren't these adorable?"

I follow her gaze to a display of delicate glass figurines. "They're beautiful," I agree. "We should each pick one out. You know, to commemorate the evening."

Sadie's eyes light up at the suggestion. "I love that idea! Okay, you choose one for me, and I'll choose one for you."

We spend the next few minutes carefully examining the ornaments, each of us trying to find the perfect one for the other. Finally, I select a tiny book for Sadie, while she chooses a miniature ice skate for me.

"It's perfect," I say softly as she hands me the ornament. Our fingers brush as I take it, and I feel a jolt of electricity at the contact.

"Just like tonight," Sadie replies, her voice equally soft.

The night is winding down, and couples and families are gathering near the outdoor screen that's been set up for the annual showing of "It's a Wonderful Life." Sadie and I are just about to settle onto a plush blanket, steaming cups of cider in hand, when a familiar voice calls out to us.

"Well, if it isn't Benton Falls' favorite couple!" Mrs. Henderson approaches, her silver curls bouncing with each step. Her eyes twinkle behind her glasses as she beams at us. "You two are just the cutest thing I've ever seen."

I feel a blush creeping up my neck at her words. "Oh, we're... I mean, thank you Mrs. Henderson," I stammer, wondering how in the heck the town gossip, sweet intentioned as she is, already knows about Sadie and my relationship upgrade.

Mrs. Henderson waves a dismissive hand. "The two of you were always just a matter of time. I know true love when I see it. You two remind me so much of Ren's parents, you know. Childhood friends who became high school sweethearts. Now that was a love story for the ages —" she stops, her smiles melt into a frown as she must remember the ending of my parent's tragic love story.

Her words hit me like a ton of bricks, bringing back a flood of memories I've tried so hard to suppress. The shouting matches, the slamming doors, the bitter custody battles... Every fear I have about relationships comes rushing back with the force of a tidal wave. I look at Sadie, panic rising in my chest as I see our future laid out before me—the inevitable arguments, the growing resentment, the painful goodbyes.

It's too much and I'm a freaking police officer. I can't have a breakdown in the middle of the Christmas market —my reputation would be ruined. "I... I can't," I choke out, my voice tight with anxiety. Sadie's eyes widen in confusion and hurt as I take a stumbling step backward. "What if this is a mistake?"

"Ren?" Sadie's voice is laced with concern. "What are you talking about?"

But I can't bring myself to explain. The words stick in my throat, choked by fear and doubt. Before she can say anything else, before I can see the tears I know are forming in her eyes, I turn and run. I push through the crowd, ignoring the startled exclamations and concerned looks. All I can focus on is the need to get away, to escape the suffocating weight of expectations and fears.

I find myself running through the festive streets of Benton Falls, leaving the Christmas market and city park behind. The cheerful decorations and twinkling lights now seem to mock me. The happiness I felt moments ago has been replaced by a gnawing fear that history is doomed to repeat itself. My parents' failed marriage, the pain it caused, the way it tore our family apart—it all plays on a loop in my mind.

As I run, chest heaving and heart pounding, I catch glimpses of my reflection in storefront windows. The fear in my eyes, the tension in my jaw—I barely recognize myself. How did I let things get this far? How could I risk my friendship with Sadie, the most important relationship in my life, for something as uncertain as romance?

I finally come to a stop at the edge of town, collapsing onto a snow-covered bench. The frigid air burns my lungs as I gulp in ragged breaths, my mind racing as fast as my heart. I've never felt more scared or vulnerable in my life. The joy and magic of the winter festival seem a distant memory now, replaced by a cold, creeping dread.

As I sit there, shivering and alone, I can't help but wonder: Have I just made the biggest mistake of my life? Or have I saved myself—and Sadie—from inevitable heartbreak? The answers elude me, lost in the swirling snow and the echoes of carols carried on the wind.

The twinkling lights of the Christmas market in the city park shine in the distance, a reminder of the warmth and happiness I've left behind. But the shadows of my fears loom larger, leaving me paralyzed with indecision. As the clock in the town square chimes midnight, marking the arrival of Christmas Eve, I'm left with a crushing realization: I have no idea what to do next.

Twenty-One

ARTHUR

Well, if this isn't just tinsel-tastic.

Here I am, standing at the edge of Benton Falls' city park, surrounded by the remnants of what was supposed to be a magical Christmas market. The twinkling lights are still up, but they're about as cheerful as a wilted poinsettia right now. All because one lovesick police officer decided to do his best impression of a startled deer and bolt.

My chest tightens as I replay the scene in my mind. Ren, looking like he'd been haunted by the ghost of Christmas past, stumbling away from Sadie. And there's Sadie, sweet Sadie, standing alone with tears glistening on her cheeks like the world's saddest Christmas ornament.

I shake my head, my long white beard swaying with the motion. "Humans," I mutter under my breath. "Give me a garden any day. At least plants don't run away from their problems."

But even as I grumble, I can feel a tug in my chest

that has nothing to do with celestial indigestion. These two knuckleheads, Ren and Sadie, have somehow managed to worm their way into my heart. Me, Arthur, the man who his earthly life digging in the dirt and talking to plants, just to avoid human interaction.

I pace the park's edge, glancing between Sadie, who's still doing her best impression of a sad snow woman, and the direction Ren disappeared. The scent of hot apple cider and cinnamon drifts towards me, a cruel reminder of the festive joy that now seems as out of place as a penguin in the Sahara.

"Oh, for heaven's sake," I grumble, torn between going to Sadie to comfort her or chasing after Ren to shake some sense into him—and possibly relieving some of my frustration.

But as I watch Sadie wrap her arms around herself, a sob finally escaping her lips, I feel something shift within me. This isn't just about my assignment or earning my wings anymore. These two young souls have become more important to me than I'd like to admit.

With a sigh, I make my decision. "Sorry, Sadie," I mutter, send up a silent plea and hope someone will come to comfort her soon. "Looks like I've got a runaway Romeo to catch."

And just like that, I see an angel appear—intuitively I know who this woman is. I feel the love Jane has for her granddaughter. She wraps her arms around Sadie, and I send up a silent prayer of gratitude. If humans only knew how many angels were waiting to answer their prayers—

ERICA PENROD

all they have to do is ask and God will send an army if necessary.

Reassured I've left Sadie in the arms of an angel, I set off in search of Ren, my angelic senses tingling, leading me through the streets like some sort of divine navigation system. I pass by storefronts decked out in enough tinsel to wrap up the entire town square.

As I walk, I can't help but reflect on the irony of the situation. Here I am, an angel who's spent centuries avoiding human entanglements, now neck-deep in a romantic crisis. If the other angels could see me now, they'd laugh their halos off.

"I hope this is worth it, Arthur," I mutter to myself. "Trading in your pruning shears for a guardian's wings. What's next? Hosting a celestial dating show?"

I finally spot Ren outside the library, hunched over on a bench like he's trying to fold himself into origami. Poor kid looks about as miserable as a snowman in July.

I plop down next to him, folding my arms over my chest. "Well, aren't you a sorry sight," I say, bypassing any heavenly platitudes. "You know, when I was your age, we didn't run away from our problems. Mainly because we were too busy running away from the vacuum cleaner sales associate, but still."

Ren looks up at me, his eyes redder than Rudolph's nose. "Arthur? What are you doing here?"

I raise an eyebrow. "What, did you think I'd let you sulk out here alone? I may be old, but I'm not heartless. Besides, someone's got to knock some sense into that thick skull of yours."

Ren winces. "So, you know what happened?"

I nod. "Yeah," I sigh. "I was at the park."

Part of me thinks this is a good opportunity to tell Ren the truth about who I am, but before I get the chance, he continues. "I really messed up, didn't I?"

"Oh, spectacularly," I nod, not one to sugarcoat things. "I haven't seen a disaster like that since Noah forgot to waterproof the ark. What were you thinking, leaving Sadie alone like that? It wasn't very gentlemanly, you know. I half expected to see your great grandmother Ellen appear and box your ears."

"What?" Ren looks at me like I've just announced aliens exist, which I didn't, now angels on the other hand... "How do you..." His forehead creases, "I didn't know my great grandma Ellen."

Well, she knows you, I think to myself. "Anyway," I continue. "You know you were just demoted to the naughty list."

Ren's face crumples like a badly wrapped present. "I know, I feel terrible. I just... I panicked."

"Clearly," I say dryly. "I've seen less panic in a candy cane factory when the sugar runs out. Care to explain what caused this festive fiasco?"

Ren explains, stumbling over his words like a snowshoer in deep drifts. I listen, resisting the urge to shake my head at the familiar tale of human fears and insecurities. Mrs. Henderson's well-meaning but triggering comments, the painful memories of his parents' divorce, the fear of repeating their mistakes—it's like a greatest hits album of relationship anxieties.

"Let me get this straight," I interrupt. "You're afraid of hurting Sadie, so your solution was to... hurt Sadie? Boy, they sure don't teach logic like they used to."

Ren looks like he's been smacked with a Christmas tree. "When you put it that way..."

"Yeah, when I put it that way, it sounds pretty ridiculous, doesn't it?" I say, but my tone softens. "Look, kid. Love isn't a garden where you can predict every bloom. It's more like... well, it's like trying to wrangle a bunch of hyperactive cherubs. Unpredictable, sometimes messy, but ultimately worth it."

Ren cracks a small smile at that. "You have experience with hyperactive cherubs?"

"You have no idea," I mutter, thinking back to some particularly chaotic days in heaven. "The point is, you can't let fear of what might happen stop you from embracing what's right in front of you."

I watch as Ren absorbs this, his face going through more expressions than a mood ring. "But what if I mess it all up?" he asks, voice trembling like a leaf in a snowstorm.

I place a hand on his shoulder, channeling a bit of heavenly warmth through the touch. "Kid, let me tell you something. You've known Sadie since you were both knee high to a grasshopper, right?"

Ren nods, looking confused.

"And in all that time, has she ever run screaming for the hills because of your various mishaps and mess-ups?"

He shakes his head slowly.

"Exactly," I say, tapping the side of my nose. "That

girl knows you better than you know yourself. She's stuck around this long, hasn't she? You think she'd do that if she didn't care about you more than a bee cares about flowers?"

A spark of hope flickers in Ren's eyes. "I... I guess not."

"You're darn right she wouldn't," I nod sagely. "Now, I'm not saying it's going to be easy. You made quite a mess back there, and it might take some time for her to forgive you. Heck, it might take a Christmas miracle. But I've got faith in you, kid. And more importantly, I've got faith in Sadie's ability to see past your momentary bout of idiocy."

Ren actually chuckles at that, the sound as welcome as a warm fire on a cold night. "Thanks, Arthur. I don't know how you always know what to say, but I'm glad you're here."

I feel a warmth spread through me that has nothing to do with my celestial nature and everything to do with the fact that I actually like this human. Heaven help me.

"Yeah, well, don't go spreading it around," I grumble good-naturedly. "I've got a reputation to maintain. Now, what are you going to do?"

Ren takes a deep breath, his shoulders straightening as he makes a decision. He looks at me with newfound determination in his eyes. "I need to fix this," he says, his voice stronger now. "First thing in the morning, I'm going to go to Sadie and apologize. I'll explain everything."

"Hallelujah, he sees the light," I say, throwing my

hands up dramatically. "And here I was worried I'd have to resort to divine intervention. Or worse, relationship advice from cupid. That guy's aim is terrible, you know."

Ren stands up, brushing off his jeans. "I should get home," he says, sounding exhausted—too exhausted to catch any of angel humor, but more centered than before. "Got a big day tomorrow."

I nod, rising to stand beside him. "Get some rest, Ren. And remember—honesty and openness. That's the key. Oh, and maybe a big present. Can't hurt to grease the wheels a bit."

As Ren walks away, looking more determined than dejected now, I can't help but smile. Henry had me worried, but I handled it.

At least I think I did.

I look up into the starry sky and send up a little prayer. Not for my wings, not this time, but for Ren and Sadie. Because sometimes, even angels need to believe in the magic of Christmas miracles—which is a good thing, because unbeknownst to me, tomorrow I was going to need one.

Twenty-Two

REN

I wake with a start, the first rays of Christmas Eve sunlight filtering through my curtains. My heart is racing, and for a moment, I can't remember why. Then it all comes rushing back—the Christmas market, Mrs. Henderson's words, my panic, and worst of all, Sadie's tear-streaked face as I ran away like a coward.

Guilt washes over me, threatening to drag me back under the covers. But I shake it off, determination taking its place. I made a mess of things last night, but I'm going to fix it. I have to. The thought of spending Christmas with this rift between Sadie and me is unbearable.

I grab my phone from the nightstand, my fingers fumbling as I dial Sadie's number. It rings once, twice, then goes straight to voicemail. My stomach drops, but I try to stay positive. Maybe she's just still asleep.

"Hey, Sadie," I say, trying to keep my voice steady. "It's me. Ren. I... I'm so sorry about last night. Can we talk? Please call me back when you get this."

I hang up, staring at the phone as if I can will it to ring. When it remains stubbornly silent, I type out a text message.

"Sadie, I know I messed up. I panicked and I'm sorry. Please give me a chance to explain. Can we meet?"

I hit send and wait, counting the seconds. One minute passes. Then five. Then ten. My anxiety grows with each passing moment. Unable to sit still any longer, I send another message.

"I understand if you're angry. You have every right to be. But please, Sadie. Don't shut me out. Not today. Not on Christmas Eve."

Still no response. The silence is deafening, and I can feel panic creeping in again. But this time, instead of running away, I'm going to face it head-on. I jump out of bed, hastily pulling on a pair of jeans and a warm sweater. The wool is scratchy against my skin, but I barely notice as I rush out the door.

The cold morning air hits me like a slap to the face as I step outside. My breath forms little clouds in front of me as I jog down the sidewalk towards Sadie's apartment. The streets of Benton Falls are quiet this early on Christmas Eve, the only sound the crunch of frost under my feet.

I reach Sadie's building in record time, my heart pounding as I climb the stairs to her second-floor apartment. I knock on her door; the sound echoing in the empty hallway. "Sadie?" I call out, trying to keep my voice down so as not to disturb her neighbors. "It's me. Can we talk?"

Silence. I knock again, a little louder this time. Still nothing. A knot forms in my stomach as I peek through the small window next to her door. The apartment is dark, no sign of movement inside.

Dejected, I make my way back down to the street. Where could she be? The library. Of course. Even on Christmas Eve, Sadie would probably be at work, losing herself in books to avoid dealing with... well, with me.

I practically run to the Evergreen Library, my feet carrying me automatically down the familiar path. The grand facade of the building comes into view, its red brick and stone walls a comforting sight. But as I reach for the heavy oak doors, I realize they're locked. A small sign in the window catches my eye: "Closed for Christmas Eve and Christmas Day. Happy Holidays!"

My heart sinks. I cup my hands around my eyes, peering through the windows. The library is dark and still, no sign of Sadie or anyone else inside. The knot in my stomach tightens. Where else could she be?

I wander through town, my mind racing. Could she have gone to her parents' house early for the holidays? No, she always insists on staying in Benton Falls until Christmas morning. Did she go to a friend's place? But who? As her best friend, I'm usually the one she turns to when she's upset.

The irony of that thought isn't lost on me. Some best friend I turned out to be.

As I walk, the town slowly comes to life around me. Shopkeepers open their doors, hanging wreaths and setting out signs advertising last-minute Christmas sales.

The scent of fresh-baked goods wafts from the bakery, mingling with the fresh pine scent of Christmas trees. Normally, these sights and smells would fill me with joy, but today they only serve as a painful reminder of the happiness I might have lost.

I find myself in the middle of the town square, surrounded by twinkling lights and festive decorations. The clock on the courthouse tower chimes nine, the sound echoing across the square. I stop in my tracks, suddenly overwhelmed by the enormity of what I've done.

Bowing my head, I close my eyes and do something I haven't done in a long time. I pray.

"God," I whisper, feeling foolish, but desperate enough to try anything. "I know I messed up. I let my fears get the best of me, and I hurt the person I care about most in the world. I'm sorry. Please... please help me find Sadie. Help me make this right. And... and if it's not too much to ask, give me the strength to be the man she deserves. To have faith in our love, even when I'm scared. Amen."

I open my eyes, half-expecting to see Sadie standing in front of me. Of course, she isn't. But I do feel a strange sense of calm wash over me. It's not much, but it's enough to keep me going.

I start walking again, no real destination in mind. My feet carry me to the park where Sadie and I have spent countless hours over the years. As I round a bend in the path, I spot a familiar figure sitting on a bench. It's Arthur, and suddenly I feel a little more hopeful.

He looks up as I approach, a serene smile on his face. "You look like you could use some help," he says, his blue eyes twinkling.

"You could say that." I let out a humorless laugh. "I can't find Sadie."

"I know." Arthur's smile widens. "I'm the angel sent to help you."

I blink, sure I must have misheard him. "I'm sorry, what?"

"An angel," he repeats calmly. "Sent to guide you on your journey."

For a moment, I'm speechless. Then I burst out laughing. It's not funny, not really, but the absurdity of the situation, combined with my frayed nerves, pushes me over the edge. "Angel, tooth fairy, I don't care," I manage to say between chuckles. "If you can help me find Sadie and win her back, I'm in."

Arthur doesn't seem offended by my laughter. Instead, he places a hand on my shoulder, his expression turning serious. "Slow down," he says gently. "Think about the girl you love. Where would she be if she's always been there for you, never letting you down?"

His words cut through my panic, forcing me to take a deep breath. I close my eyes, thinking about Sadie. About all the times she's been there for me, supporting me through thick and thin. About her unwavering loyalty, her kindness, her strength.

And suddenly, I know.

I know exactly where she is.

My eyes fly open, and I look at Arthur with

newfound gratitude. "I have to go," I say urgently. "Thank you."

I take off running, calling back over my shoulder, "Merry Christmas!" As I sprint down the sidewalk, my heart is pounding, but this time it's with hope and determination. I know where Sadie is, and I know what I need to do.

As I run, the words of my prayer echo in my mind. I may not understand how, but I can't shake the feeling that somehow, in some way, it's been answered. Whether Arthur is really an angel or just a kind old man with good advice doesn't matter. What matters is that I've been given a second chance, and I'm not going to waste it.

The cold air burns in my lungs as I run, but I barely notice. All I can think about is Sadie, and the look on her face when I find her. Will she be angry? Hurt? Will she even want to see me? I push the doubts aside. It doesn't matter. I'll do whatever it takes to make this right.

As I round the final corner, my destination comes into view. Of course. How could I have forgotten? This is where our story began, all those years ago. And if I have anything to say about it, this is where our new chapter will start.

With a silent prayer of thanks — to God, to Arthur, to whatever forces brought me here—I take a deep breath and step forward. It's time to face the music, to confront my fears, and to fight for the love I've been too afraid to claim.

Because Sadie isn't just my best friend. She's the love of my life. And I can't lose her now.

Twenty-Three

I round the corner, the chilly December air nipping at my skin as my breath comes in white puffs. I'm pretty sure I've set a new personal record for "most dramatic run through town," and I make a mental note to add "fleeing from emotional conversations" to my workout routine.

The familiar red brick building of Benton Falls Elementary School looms before me, its windows adorned with paper snowflakes and twinkling lights. My heart races, and not just from the run. This is it. This is where I'll find Sadie. I just hope she hasn't turned into a human popsicle waiting for me to get my act together.

As I approach the school, memories flood back. Sadie and I spent countless hours on this playground, from our first day of kindergarten to our last day of fifth grade. It was here, on a swing set, much like the one I can see now, that we made our childhood pact to be best friends forever. The irony of that promise isn't lost on me as I scan the snow-covered playground, searching for her. I half expect to see "Ren is a dummy" written in the snow. It would be well-deserved.

And then I see her.

Sadie sits on one swing, her slender figure hunched against the cold. Her chestnut hair spills out from beneath a knit cap, and even from here, I can see the redness of her nose and cheeks. She looks small and vulnerable, and my heart clenches knowing that I'm the reason she's out here in the freezing cold on Christmas Eve. I'm officially the worst best friend since Judas.

I approach slowly; the snow crunching beneath my boots. Sadie looks up as I near, and the mix of emotions that flicker across her face — relief, frustration, hope, hurt — nearly stops me in my tracks. But I keep moving forward. I've run away once; I won't do it again. Besides, my legs are too tired for another sprint.

"Took you long enough," Sadie says as I come to a stop a few feet away. Despite the tension in her voice, I catch a hint of a smile, and it gives me hope. "I was thinking I'd have to put out an APB on you. 'Missing: One emotionally stunted police officer. Last seen fleeing from happiness.'"

I wince at her words, but I can't argue with them. "Why are you out here in the cold on Christmas Eve?" I ask, unable to keep the concern from my voice. My hands itch to reach out and warm her up, but I hold back, unsure if my touch would be welcome. Knowing my luck, she'd probably think I was trying to check her for weapons or something.

Sadie shrugs, her breath forming little clouds in the air. "I didn't think I'd be out here that long. I figured you'd find me sooner." Her words are matter-of-fact, but I can hear the undercurrent of hurt, and it cuts me to the core. "Though I have to say, waiting out here has given me a new appreciation for polar bears. Think the zoo is hiring?"

I sigh, my shoulders slumping under the weight of my regret. "I've been slow on a lot of things," I admit, my voice thick with emotion. "I'm so sorry for running out on you last night, Sadie. I was scared and stupid. Which, come to think of it, is a pretty accurate description of me most of the time."

Sadie watches me, her hazel eyes softening but still guarded. I take a deep breath, knowing that this is my moment. If I'm going to fix this, if I'm going to have any chance of salvaging not just our friendship but the possibility of something more, I need to lay it all out there. No pressure or anything.

"I've been such an idiot, Sadie," I begin, the words tumbling out. "I've been so scared of losing our friendship that I almost threw it away. When Mrs. Henderson started talking about how we reminded her of my parents, all I could think about was how their marriage ended. How they went from best friends to barely speaking. I panicked. I think I set a new land speed record for 'man fleeing from emotional vulnerability.'"

I run a hand through my hair, frustrated with myself. "But I realize now that I was looking at it all wrong. My parents' story isn't our story. And even if it was, running

163

away isn't the answer. You deserve better than that. You deserve someone who will stand by you, no matter what. Someone who won't bolt at the first sign of feelings like a scared rabbit."

Sadie's eyes glisten with unshed tears, and I ache to reach out and wipe them away. But she needs to say her piece, so I wait, feeling like the world's most anxious statue.

"It hurt to have you run out on me," she says quietly, her voice barely above a whisper. "But most of all, my best friend would never do that to me. I need to know you won't do that again. If you can't handle us being more than friends, I need to know now. I can't lose you. Though I might consider investing in a leash if you're planning on making running away a habit."

Her words hit me like a physical blow, but I can't help but chuckle at her last comment. Leave it to Sadie to inject humor into even the most serious moments. It's one thing I love most about her.

I step closer; the snow crunching under my boots. "I finally understand, Sadie," I say, my voice low and earnest. "I'm not trading our friendship for a romance. Our friendship is the foundation of everything. It's an integral part of the love I have for you. And let's face it, you're the only one who puts up with my terrible jokes and questionable taste in movies."

Sadie's eyes search my face, looking for the truth in my words. I reach out and take her hands in mine, feeling the coldness of her skin. "I promise," I say, pouring every ounce of sincerity I possess into my words. "I will always be your best friend and the man who loves you. I won't run away again. Unless you decide to make me watch 'The Notebook' for the hundredth time. Then all bets are off."

Tears well up in Sadie's eyes, but this time, they're accompanied by a smile—a genuine, heartfelt smile that makes my chest tighten with emotion. "I needed to hear that," she whispers, squeezing my hands. "And for the record, 'The Notebook' is a cinematic masterpiece. Your taste in movies really is questionable."

Unable to resist any longer, I pull her into a hug, wrapping my arms around her and holding her close. The coldness of the air fades away as we stand there, connected and secure in each other's embrace. "I love you, Sadie," I murmur into her hair, breathing in the familiar scent of her shampoo mixed with the crisp winter air. "Even if you do have terrible taste in movies."

Sadie burrows deeper into my arms, her voice muffled against my chest. "I love you too, Ren. I have for so long. Despite your emotional constipation and your weird obsession with action movies."

We stand like that for a long moment, neither of us willing to let go. When we finally do separate, Sadie's cheeks are flushed, and not just from the cold. She looks up at me with a mix of joy and mischief in her eyes.

"You know," she says, a playful lilt in her voice, "for a police officer, you're not very observant. I've been dropping hints for years. I was thinking I'd need to hire a skywriter or something."

I laugh, the sound echoing across the empty playground. "Well, for a librarian, you could have been a bit more direct with your storytelling," I tease back. "Maybe next time try, 'See Ren Run. See Ren Love Sadie. See Sadie Knock Some Sense Into Ren.'"

Hand in hand, we make our way to the swing set. As we sit down, the chains creak in protest, reminding us we're not the small children who used to play here. "I think the swing set is trying to tell us we're too old for this," I chuckle.

"Speak for yourself," Sadie retorts. "I'm as spry as ever. Watch this!" She attempts to pump her legs to gain height, but only manages a pitiful sway. "Okay, maybe the swing set has a point."

As snowflakes fall gently around us, I feel the same sense of wonder and possibility that I did as a kid. Only now, it's mixed with a healthy dose of adult awkwardness and the realization that my butt is definitely too big for this swing.

"Do you remember the day we met?" Sadie asks, her feet scuffing at the thin layer of snow beneath the swing.

I nod, a smile tugging at my lips. "How could I forget? First day of kindergarten. You marched right up to me and declared that we were going to be best friends. I thought you were some kind of tiny, pigtailed dictator."

Sadie laughs, the sound like music to my ears. "And you looked at me like I was crazy."

"Can you blame me? You were missing your two front teeth and had pigtails sticking out at odd angles," I tease. "You looked like a tiny, very enthusiastic scarecrow."

She bumps her shoulder against mine. "Hey, I'll have you know those pigtails were very fashionable. I was ahead of my time."

"Sure, if your time was the 'disheveled farm girl' era," I quip, earning myself another shoulder bump.

We laugh together, the tension of the past day melting away like snow in the sun. As our laughter subsides, a comfortable silence falls between us. The snow continues to fall, transforming the playground into a winter wonderland. Christmas lights from nearby houses twinkle through the trees, casting a magical glow over everything.

"Sadie," I say softly, turning to face her. "I want you to know that I meant every word I said. You're my best friend, and that will never change. But you're also so much more than that. You're the person I want to share every day with, every adventure, every quiet moment. You're the one I want to build a future with. Even if that future involves way too many romantic comedies and not enough explosions in our movie nights."

Sadie's eyes shimmer with tears, but her smile is radiant. "That sounds an awful lot like a proposal, Officer Michaels," she says, her tone light but her eyes serious. "Should I be checking your pockets for a ring, or did you leave that in your other pants when you were busy running away from your feelings?"

I feel a blush creep up my neck, but I don't back down. "Maybe it is," I say, my heart pounding. "Not an official one—I think we both deserve something a little more romantic than a snowy playground for that. Plus,

I'd probably manage to drop the ring in the snow and we'd spend our engagement digging for it. But consider it a promise. A promise that I'm all in, Sadie. For friendship, for love, for everything. Even for your weird obsession with color-coding your bookshelf."

Sadie leans in, pressing her forehead against mine. "I like the sound of that promise," she whispers. "And for the record, color-coding is a perfectly valid organizational system. You're just jealous because your idea of organizing is 'throw everything in a drawer and hope for the best.'"

As we sit there, our breaths mingling in the cold air, I silently thank whatever forces brought us to this moment. I think of Arthur, the mysterious old man who seemed to appear just when I needed guidance. Was he really an angel sent to help me see what was right in front of me all along? Or just a kind stranger with good advice? At this moment, it doesn't matter. What matters is that I'm here, with Sadie, on the precipice of something wonderful. And if Arthur is an angel, I hope he's got a good sense of humor, because he's going to need it dealing with us.

The town clock chimes in the distance, reminding us it's getting late on Christmas Eve. But neither of us moves to leave. Instead, we sit on the swings, talking and laughing, sharing stories and dreams for the future. The cold doesn't bother us anymore, warmed as we are by each other's presence and the glow of newfound love.

As the snow falls gently around us, transforming the playground into a scene from a Christmas card, I know that this moment, this connection, is the true magic of Christmas. It's not about presents or decorations, but about the love we share with the people who matter most. Even if those people drive us crazy sometimes with their movie choices and organizational habits.

I look at Sadie, her cheeks rosy from the cold and her eyes bright with happiness, and I know that I've received the greatest gift of all. A best friend, a partner, a love that's been years in the making. And as we eventually stand to leave, hand in hand, I silently vow to cherish this gift for all the Christmases to come.

And maybe, just maybe, I'll let her color-code my sock drawer. It's the least I can do after all the running I've put her through.

Twenty-Four

REN

I step into the twinkling town square, already bustling with Christmas Eve revelers, and inhale the winter air. The scent of pine drifts through the air, mingling with the mouthwatering aroma of roasted chestnuts and freshly baked gingerbread. All around me, the sounds of laughter and cheerful chatter blend with the distant strains of "Jingle Bells" played by a brass quartet near the giant Christmas tree. I can't help but grin, eager for the evening's magic.

Benton Falls is the embodiment of Christmas magic. The majestic clock tower at the center of the square stands as a beacon of elegance, its classic stone facade and intricate carvings illuminated by soft, warm light. The four clock faces, framed by ornate ironwork, seem to glow against the night sky. Strings of twinkling lights crisscross overhead, casting a golden glow over the cobblestone streets and the faces of my friends and neighbors.

In one corner of the square, the town's grand Christmas tree stands proudly, its branches laden with twinkling lights and ornaments crafted by local children. Across from the tree, a stage has been set up for Christmas performances, where a group of carolers is preparing to entertain the crowd. On the opposite side, I can see a couple of cozy food stands offering hot chocolate and an array of Christmas goodies, their inviting aromas making my mouth water.

As I take in the festive scene, a warm hand clasps mine. I look down to see Sadie by my side, her eyes sparkling with joy. My heart skips a beat at her radiant smile. She's bundled up in a cozy red sweater, a white knit scarf wrapped snugly around her neck. Snowflakes have settled in her chestnut hair, making her look like she's wearing a diamond-studded crown.

"No getting lost in the crowd this year, Sades," I murmur, giving her fingers a gentle squeeze. "I'm not letting you out of my sight tonight."

Sadie's cheeks flush a pretty pink, and she leans into me, her warmth seeping through my jacket. "Promise?" she asks, her voice soft and full of meaning.

"Cross my heart," I reply, drawing an X over my chest with my free hand. "You're stuck with me."

Her eyes sparkle with mischief. "I'll hold you to it."

Hand in hand, we begin to wander through the holiday market. The festive stalls lining the square offer everything from handcrafted ornaments to steaming cups of hot chocolate. The air is alive with the mingled scents of sweet and savory treats, making my mouth water.

At a confectionery stand, we sample decadent truffles that melt on our tongues, leaving behind a rich, velvety sweetness. The vendor, a jolly man with rosy cheeks that remind me of Santa Claus, offers us cups of mulled cider. The warm, spiced drink sends tendrils of heat through my body, chasing away the winter chill.

As we move from stall to stall, I can't help but marvel at how different this feels from our previous Christmas Eves together. There's a new intimacy in the way Sadie leans into me, in how our hands remain intertwined even as we browse. It's as if the shift in our relationship has added a layer of magic to an already enchanting night.

At one of the craft stalls, a kitschy reindeer ornament catches my eye. It's wearing a tiny police uniform, complete with a miniature badge. I can't resist buying it for Sadie, presenting it to her with a flourish.

"To commemorate the night Officer Rudolph finally got his act together," I say with a wink.

Sadie laughs, the sound like music to my ears. She takes the ornament, admiring it with a soft smile. "It's perfect," she says, her eyes meeting mine. "Though I hope you're not planning on growing a red nose to match."

As she speaks, I notice a smudge of powdered sugar on her upper lip, likely from the beignet she'd sampled earlier. Without thinking, I reach out, gently brushing it away with my thumb. The simple touch sends a jolt of electricity through me, and I find myself frozen, my hand cupping her cheek.

Sadie's eyes widen, her breath catching. For a moment, we stand there, lost in each other's gaze. Then, with a soft smile, she reaches up, mirroring my gesture. Her fingers are warm against my skin as she brushes away what I assume is errant icing sugar dotting my lips.

"Always looking out for me," I murmur, turning my head slightly to press a kiss to her palm.

"Someone has to," she teases, but her voice is tender.

We're pulled from our moment by the sound of carolers striking up "Silent Night." Their soaring harmonies raise goosebumps on my arms, the beauty of the song filling the air around us. Without a word, I pull Sadie close, swaying with her in a gentle makeshift dance.

As we move together, the first snowflakes of the evening drift down, adding to the magical atmosphere. They catch in Sadie's eyelashes, making her eyes seem to sparkle even more than usual. I'm struck by how beautiful she is, how perfect this moment feels.

Breathless with wonder, Sadie tilts her face up, letting the icy kisses melt on her tongue. I watch her with unabashed adoration, my heart swelling with love. This is the girl I've known almost my entire life, my best friend, and now, somehow, impossibly, something even more.

"What?" Sadie asks, noticing my intense gaze.

I shake my head, smiling. "Just thinking about how lucky I am," I admit. "And how I almost let my fears keep me from this."

Sadie's expression softens. She reaches up, cupping my face in her hands. "But you didn't," she says firmly. "You're here now. We're here now. That's what matters."

ERICA PENROD

I nod, leaning down to rest my forehead against hers. We stay like that for a long moment, swaying gently to the music, the snow falling softly around us. It feels like we're in our own little bubble, separate from the bustling crowd around us.

As midnight approaches, the crowd gravitates toward the massive evergreen dominating the town square. It's a Benton Falls tradition—gathering around the tree at midnight on Christmas Eve to light candles and sing carols. Sadie and I join the throng, our hands clasped tightly together.

Mayor Evelyn Green steps up to a small lectern, her silver-gray bob gleaming in the soft light of the square. Her bright blue eyes sparkle as she surveys the crowd, a warm smile on her face. She's dressed in a festive red sweater and black slacks, looking both professional and approachable.

"Friends, neighbors, welcome to our annual Christmas Eve celebration," she begins, her voice ringing out over the square. "As we stand here together, let us remember the true spirit of this season — love, joy, and community."

She speaks about coming together, of supporting one another through good times and bad. As she talks, I feel a lump forming in my throat. Her words resonate deeply, reminding me of how close I came to pushing away the most important person in my life.

When she finishes her speech, volunteers move through the crowd, lighting candles. Soon, the entire square is bathed in a warm, flickering glow. The sight is

174

breathtaking — hundreds of tiny flames illuminating the night, a sea of light against the darkness.

As the first notes of "O Holy Night" begin to play, I glance up, only to find myself and Sadie haloed beneath a swath of mistletoe. My pulse thunders in my ears as our eyes lock with electric intensity. In that moment, everything else fades away—the crowd, the music, even the gently falling snow. All I can see is Sadie, her face illuminated by candlelight, her eyes shining with love.

"Sadie...I..." My words catch in my throat as my thumb traces the curve of her lips with infinite tenderness. Everywhere our skin meets, heat blossoms. I'm overwhelmed by the depth of my feelings for her, by the realization that this is real, that we're really here.

"You're everything to me, Sadie," I rasp, my voice thick with barely restrained emotion. "I don't want to imagine a life without you in it."

Tears well up in Sadie's eyes, but she's smiling. "You don't have to," she whispers. "I'm not going anywhere, Ren. Not ever."

In that transcendent instant, every ghost, every fear, every stumbling block melts away into insignificance. Sadie is my destiny—the one who has been there all along, and our love is so much stronger, built on the foundation of friendship. I don't know why I ever thought I had to choose between friendship and love. It's Christmas, the season of gifts and miracles, and with Sadie, I have it all.

So when I cradle her face in my hands and seal our connection with the softest, sweetest kiss imaginable, it feels less like discovery and more like...reclamation. Coming home at long last to where I've always belonged —safe in the shelter of Sadie's infinite devotion.

The kiss is tender, full of promise and shared history. When we finally part, both of us are a little breathless. Sadie's eyes are shining, and I can feel the widest grin spreading across my face.

"Merry Christmas, Ren," Sadie murmurs, her fingers playing with the hair at the nape of my neck.

"Merry Christmas, Sades," I reply, pulling her close for another quick kiss.

As we stand there, wrapped in each other's arms, the church bells chime in the distance, signaling the arrival of Christmas Day. The sound rings out across the square, clear and joyful, perfectly capturing the feeling in my heart.

I glance around, taking in the scene. The candlelit faces of our friends and neighbors, the gently falling snow, the twinkling lights—it's like something out of a dream. My gaze lands on a familiar figure standing at the edge of the crowd, and I feel a jolt of surprise.

It's Arthur, the kindly old man who's given me so much guidance over the past few weeks. He's watching us with a warm smile, his blue eyes twinkling. As our eyes meet, he gives me a nod and a wave. Then, to my astonishment, he seems to shimmer slightly before disappearing into thin air.

I blink, sure I must be seeing things. But no—- the spot where Arthur stood is now empty, with no sign that he was ever there.

"Ren? What is it?" Sadie asks, noticing my distraction.

I shake my head, smiling. "Nothing," I say, turning back to her. "Just... thinking that maybe miracles really happen at Christmas."

Sadie laughs, snuggling closer to me. "I'd say so," she agrees. "After all, you finally figured out how you feel about me. If that's not a Christmas miracle, I don't know what is."

I chuckle, pressing a kiss to the top of her head. "Hilarious," I murmur. But as I hold her close, watching the snow fall gently around us, I can't help but think that she might be right. Whoever Arthur was, he helped me see what was right in front of me all along.

And now, with Sadie in my arms and a lifetime of love stretching out before us, I know that this is just the beginning of our story.

As we join in with the crowd singing "Joy to the World," I feel a sense of peace and happiness unlike anything I've ever experienced. This is what Christmas is all about, I realize. Not just the lights and the music and the presents, but the love that binds people together. The kind of love that can overcome any obstacle, if given the chance to grow strong.

I look down at Sadie; her face glowing with happiness, and I know that I've received the greatest gift of all. A best friend, a partner, a love that's been years in the making. And as we stand there, surrounded by the magic of Christmas Eve in Benton Falls, I silently vow to cherish this gift for all the Christmases to come.

Epilogue

ARTHUR

The soft, ethereal glow of the celestial lobby envelops me as I sit, my hands clasped tightly in my lap. The ornate doors of the Grand Hall loom before me, their intricate designs seeming to shimmer and shift in the golden light that seeps through the cracks. I can feel the weight of anticipation pressing down upon me, a reminder of how much rides on this moment.

"Well, Arthur," I mutter to myself, "two years as an angel, and here you are. From tending gardens in post-war America to tending celestial ones. Talk about a career change."

I'm the only angel waiting in the lobby, which somehow makes it worse. No distractions, just me and my thoughts—not even a plant to talk to.

The air is thick with anticipation, punctuated by the distant, harmonious chiming that seems to emanate from the very fabric of Heaven itself. I breathe deeply, inhaling the subtle scent of stardust and eternity that permeates this place.

"Smells like divine anxiety with a hint of celestial butterflies," I think wryly. "Not too different from the nerves I felt on my first day at the factory back in '63."

My mind wanders back to Earth, to Benton Falls, to Ren and Sadie. Their faces flash before my eyes, and I feel a warmth spread through my chest. It's a peculiar sensation, like the time I accidentally sat on Mrs. Johnson's prize-winning tomato at the 1968 county fair, but... pleasant.

"Well, I'll be darned," I mutter to myself. "Is this what the youngsters call 'feelings'? At my age?"

It's a sensation I've become familiar with over the course of my assignment, one that I now grudgingly recognize as love. Not the mushy, hand-holding kind of love that blossomed between my two charges, *thank heavens*, but a different kind—the love of a friend, a guide, a protector. The kind of love that makes you want to shake some sense into someone and hug them at the same time.

"Who would've thought?" I chuckle internally. "Old Arthur, former curmudgeon extraordinaire, going soft over a couple of kids. What's next? Trading in my pruning shears for a harp?"

The sound of the Grand Hall doors opening snaps me back to the present. I look up to see Rose, another angel-in-training, stepping out. Her face is radiant, glowing with joy and accomplishment. A soft golden aura surrounds her, pulsing gently in time with her emotions. Henry is there to greet her, his kind eyes twinkling with pride.

"Well done, Rose," Henry says, his voice warm and full of approval. "You've truly embraced the essence of your assignment."

Rose's joy manifests as an intensification of the golden glow around her. I feel a surge of inspiration at the sight, quickly followed by a wave of panic.

Great, I think. *She's glowing like a celestial nightlight. Meanwhile, I'll probably walk in there and trip over my own robe. Wouldn't be the first time I've stumbled at a crucial moment. Remember the company picnic of '72, Arthur?*

Before I can spiral further into my anxieties, Henry turns to me. His expression is encouraging, reassuring. "It's your turn, Arthur," he says, opening the door wider.

I stand, my legs feeling surprisingly unsteady for an ethereal being. "Here goes nothing," I mutter under my breath. "Just don't mention the time you accidentally flooded the begonia section of the celestial gardens, and you'll be fine."

I take a deep breath, more out of habit than necessity, and walk towards the Grand Hall. With each step, I feel the weight of my experiences on Earth and in Heaven, the lessons learned, the friendships forged. They propel me forward, giving me strength.

As I step inside the Grand Hall, I'm momentarily awestruck by its vastness and beauty... the soft, golden glow that permeates Heaven seems to pulse here, emanating from every surface. The cool marble floor beneath my feet gleams, reflecting the light in mesmerizing patterns. The ceiling, if there is one, is lost in a swirling mist of celestial energy.

Wow, I think. *Makes my garden look like a window box. Note to self: ask about the lighting setup later.*

My eyes are drawn to the front row, where I see Saint Nicholas seated beside Henry.

Whoa. Saint Nicholas himself.

Saint Nicholas, with his flowing silvery-white hair and piercing blue eyes, exudes an aura of warmth and wisdom. His deep white robe, adorned with intricate gold embroidery, seems to shimmer with its own inner light. The sight of him is both comforting and daunting.

No pressure, Arthur, I tell myself. *It's just an arch angel. The actual celestial Saint Nicholas. Who's about to judge your worthiness. This is fine. Everything's fine.*

I make my way to the lectern, feeling the weight of countless unseen eyes upon me. The silence in the hall is profound, broken only by the soft rustling of my robe and the ever-present harmonious chiming that seems to come from everywhere and nowhere at once.

As I place my notes on the lectern, I take another deep breath. The scent of Heaven fills my lungs—a mix of starlight and eternity, with undercurrents of every beautiful fragrance known to humanity. It steadies me, reminding me of why I'm here, of the journey that has led me to this moment.

Right, I think. *Just pretend you're talking to your plants. Except these plants can talk back. And judge you. And potentially deny you your wings. No big deal.*

I spoke, my voice steady but filled with emotion. "When I was first assigned to Ren, I believed my task was simple: to help him understand the foundation of friendship. I thought I knew what that meant, but it turns out there's a big difference between pruning a heavenly rosebush and trying to untangle human emotions." I smile at my audience. *At least the rosebush doesn't run away when it sees you coming,* I add mentally.

As I talk, I notice a subtle shift in the atmosphere of the hall. A gentle scent of pine and cinnamon wafts through the air, reminiscent of the Christmas season on Earth. It brings with it memories of twinkling lights, festive markets, and the warmth of human connection.

Great, I think. *Now I'm craving gingerbread. Focus, Arthur!*

"My journey with Ren and Sadie taught me more than I could have ever imagined," I continue. "I watched as they navigated the complexities of their relationship, as they struggled with fears and insecurities, as they found the courage to be vulnerable with each other."

I recount the moments that defined my time on Earth—the conversations with Ren in the park, the quiet observations of Sadie in the library, the bustling energy of the Christmas market. With each memory, I feel a warmth spreading through me, a soft golden glow beginning to emanate from within.

Oh great, I think. *Now I'm glowing. Hopefully, it's a good glow and not a 'about to spontaneously combust' glow.*

"I saw Ren grapple with his fear of ruining his friendship with Sadie by admitting his deeper feelings. I witnessed Sadie's unwavering support and kindness, even when she was hurting. I observed as they both put each other's happiness above their own desires."

The golden glow around me intensifies as I speak, reflecting the depth of emotion in my words. I can see Henry and Saint Nicholas leaning forward slightly, their expressions attentive and thoughtful.

"And then, on that snowy Christmas Eve, I watched as they finally found the courage to embrace their love for each other. But it wasn't just romantic love I saw blossoming that night. It was the culmination of years of friendship, of trust, of mutual support and understanding."

I pause, feeling the weight of my next words. "It was then that I realized something profound. My assignment wasn't to teach Ren about friendship. It was for Ren and Sadie to teach me."

A ripple of energy passes through the hall at this admission. I can feel the surprise and interest from the unseen audience. Even Henry's eyebrows raise slightly.

"You see," I continue, my voice growing stronger with conviction, "I had always viewed friendship from a distance. I understood it intellectually, but I had never truly experienced it. Through Ren and Sadie, I learned that true friendship is about more than just being there for someone. It's about vulnerability, about taking risks, about putting someone else's happiness on par with — or even above—your own."

The golden glow around me pulses brightly as I speak, reflecting the intensity of my emotions. "I learned that friendship, at its core, is love. It's not always easy. It requires patience, understanding, and sometimes, sacrifice. But it's also one of the most rewarding experiences a being—human or angel—can have."

I look directly at Henry and Saint Nicholas as I deliver my final words. "In helping Ren and Sadie find their way to each other, I found something I didn't even know I was missing. I found friendship. And in doing so, I believe I understand one of the fundamental principles of Heaven itself—the power of love in all its forms."

As I conclude my speech, a profound silence falls over the hall. The harmonious chiming seems to have faded away, leaving only the soft pulsing of the golden light that surrounds me. I stand there, heart pounding, waiting for a response.

Well, Arthur, I think to myself. *You've done it now. Either you're getting your wings, or you're about to be assigned to prune the thorny bushes in the furthest corner of Heaven for the next millennium.*

After what feels like an eternity, Henry stands. His eyes are shining with what looks suspiciously like tears, though I didn't think angels could cry. When he speaks, his voice is warm and filled with approval.

"Arthur," he says, "when we assigned you to Ren, we

hoped you would learn something about the nature of friendship. But you've gone beyond our expectations. You've not only understood the concept, but you've also embraced it."

Huh, I think. *Maybe I have. Ren and Sadie's faces appear in my mind, and I realize how much I'm going to miss them.*

He pauses, a gentle smile playing on his lips. "You entered this assignment focused on completing a task, on earning your wings. But somewhere along the way, you forgot about the reward. You became more concerned with the well-being of your charges—your friends—than getting into Enoch's Garden. And in doing so, you've demonstrated the true essence of what it means to be a guardian angel."

A wave of emotion washes over me at Henry's words. I hadn't realized until this moment how true they were. Somewhere along the line, earning my wings had become secondary to helping Ren and Sadie find happiness.

Henry continues, his voice ringing clearly through the hall. "Because you were more concerned about your friends than your own reward, you have passed the final assignment. You've learned the true meaning of friendship, and in doing so, you have embodied the very principle you were sent to Earth to understand."

As the last word leaves Henry's lips, a heavenly bell chimes. The sound resonates through the hall, filled with divine energy. It's a sound I've heard before, but never directed at me. It's the sound of wings being bestowed.

Unexpectedly, I'm nervous. *Please don't let me botch this up. I've waited too long to trip over my new wings.*

Suddenly, I feel a weight on my back - not a burden, but a freeing, uplifting sensation. Large, beautiful celestial white wings materialize, stretching out behind me. They're not physical in the earthly sense, but a manifestation of divine energy, of the newfound understanding and love I've gained.

I feel lighter, freer, overwhelmed with joy and a sense of fulfillment. The golden glow around me brightens, pulsing in time with the beating of my metaphorical heart. It's a moment of pure, unadulterated happiness, tinged with a bittersweet realization that my time with Ren and Sadie has come to an end.

Well, I'll be a cherub's uncle, I think, awestruck. *I actually did it. Got my wings and everything. Now, how do I steer these things?*

As I stand there, marveling at this new development, Saint Nicholas rises from his seat. His eyes, as blue as the clearest sky, are filled with warmth and pride. When he speaks, his voice is deep and resonant, filled with the wisdom of ages.

"Congratulations, Arthur," he says, his words carrying the weight of divine approval. "You have not only earned your wings, but you have truly embraced the heavenly law and principle of friendship. Your journey reminds us all that even we, as celestial beings, have much to learn from the humans we guide."

I bow my head, humbled by his words. "Thank you, Saint Nicholas," I say, trying not to let my voice quaver.

"Though I have to say, I never expected to be getting life lessons from someone I used to think was just really good at breaking and entering."

Henry chuckles as Saint Nicholas tips his head and offers me a wide smile.

As the ceremony concludes and I prepare to take on my new role as a full-fledged guardian angel, my thoughts drift back to Ren and Sadie. I hope they know, on some level, how much they've given me. How much they've taught me. And I vow, in that moment, to carry the lessons of friendship they've imparted with me through all my future assignments.

As I leave the Grand Hall, my new wings shimmering behind me, I feel a sense of completion. But also, paradoxically, a sense of new beginnings. For every ending is just a new beginning in disguise. And this, I realize, is the true magic of existence—whether on Earth or in Heaven. The constant opportunity for growth, for love, for friendship.

I step out into the celestial realm, ready for whatever comes next. Because now I know—truly know—that with friendship, with love, anything is possible. And that, perhaps, is the greatest Christmas miracle of all.

Now, I think to myself as I spread my new wings, *let's see if I can avoid crashing into any clouds on my first flight. Wouldn't want to start my guardian angel career with a celestial traffic violation.*

And with that thought, I take off into the vast expanse of Heaven, ready for my next adventure—and hopefully, many new friendships along the way.

ERICA PENROD

Continue reading for a glimpse into Angel Institute Book 2: *Bailey*.

Spend more time with angels in training this Christmas!

Angel Institute Book 3

GLADYS

I bounce into the classroom, my golden curls bobbing with each step. The air crackles with excitement, and I can barely contain myself as I plop down in my chair next to John. John has wrinkles around his eyes and smile lines. He's stoic and yet has a good heart. I know this because he likes to wear socks with different designs on them. It's like, he has this hidden personality that he can't tamp down.

"Oh, gosh!" I exclaim as I accidentally knock over my pencil holder. "Sorry, sorry!" I scramble to gather the scattered pencils, offering an apologetic grin to my fellow angels-in-training. I'm one of the few angels who have anything on her desk. I like things where I can see them; they help inspire new ideas. Like this pencil holder . . . what else could it be used for? Why, the possibilities are endless.

John chuckles warmly. "Gladys, you're a whirlwind. Here, let me help you with those."

I suppose I am a whirlwind. I don't mean to be; it's just the way I was created. I can't stop it anymore that Rose can stop tap dancing. "Thanks, John. I'm just so excited. Can you believe we're finally getting our assignments?"

John nods, his eyes twinkling behind his glasses. "I know. It's a big day for all of us."

Henry, our revered instructor and mentor, clears his throat, drawing our attention to the front of the room. His majestic wings are folded neatly behind him, and his slightly messy, silver hair catches the light.

"Welcome," Henry begins, his voice warm and reassuring. He loves us. I just know it down to the bottom of my feet. Success seems so much more possible with his encouragement and desire for each of us to move on to full guardian angel status. "... Each of you will receive a letter with your final assignment on Earth."

I lean forward, hanging on his every word. Christmas on Earth! What a wonderful time of year to bring joy, love, goodness, hope, and all the feelings that Christ inspires in each of us.

Henry's tone grows more serious. "... in danger of losing Christmas Spirit forever."

Lillian, always quick to speak up, starts to ask, "That means—."

Henry nods solemnly. "It means that *you* are important in The Plan." His gaze meets each of ours in turn. "Never forget that."

I sit up straighter, feeling a swell of pride. I didn't get promoted to shift manager at the Blessings Hotline for nothing, after all. We are all important to The Plan, but today, I feel just a little bit more important than yesterday, and that's because I'll be helping someone find their way. Er–rather, not lose it completely. Lost souls are a whole other level of guardianship. Maybe one day, I'll get an advanced degree and move up, but for now, I'm more than content to help those who stand at a crossroads.

Henry continues, explaining our mission parameters. "You have until midnight on Christmas Eve to fulfill your mission, and then you'll return here to give a dissertation on your experience before an archangel. Pass, and you'll earn your wings. Fail, and you'll have to wait a hundred years before you can apply to try again."

A collective groan ripples through the room. John raises his hand, his colorful socks peeking out from under his robe as he shifts in his seat. "Is failure really possible?"

Henry's expression softens. "We have a twenty percent failure rate. It happens. Some angels fail several times. Don't be discouraged, and don't worry about what happens next. Focus on the good. Work in faith. You'll do just fine."

As Henry begins handing out the letters, I can barely sit still. I watch as my classmates receive their assignments, each reacting in their own way.

When Henry reaches me, his eyes twinkle with mischief. "Gladys, are you ready for your big adventure?"

I nod enthusiastically, nearly bouncing out of my seat. "I can't wait to see what you've got for me." I hold out my hands and wiggle my fingers.

He hands me the letter with a knowing smile. "Your creativity will serve you well for this."

As I take the letter, I feel a mix of excitement and nervousness. I say a quick prayer before opening it, my heart pounding with anticipation.

My excitement dims slightly as I read the details. "Oh, Bailey," I whisper to myself, my heart aching for her.

Rebecca, seated behind me, leans forward. "What did you get, Gladys?"

I turn to her. "I've got to help a woman named Bailey. She's having trouble connecting with others."

Rebecca nods sympathetically. "That sounds challenging. I think you'll do great, though. You like complex things."

I smile gratefully at her encouragement. "Thanks, Rebecca. What about you?"

She sighs dramatically. "All things are possible with God, right?"

"Right!" Lillian pipes up from across the aisle, her eyes sparkling with mischief. "Think I can use lollipops as bribes?"

We all laugh away the tension that has gathered inside of us as we learned the plight of our assignments.

John adjusts his colorful socks, a habit he does when he's nervous. "I'm assigned to help a kid."

I giggle. To John, everyone seems like a kid. He could have a sixty-year-old man for all I know. Hey! Maybe I'll see them. I don't know how often our assignments cross paths, but it's a possibility.

Henry dismisses us to get started, and I clutch my

assignment letter to my chest as we leave the building. I love it on campus; it's a place of learning. But I can't be an eternal student—I asked. At some point, they want you to give back. I get it; I do. And I'm ready to do my part.

"Earth, here I come," I declare, my voice filled with determination and joy. "Ready or not, Bailey, it's time to rediscover the beauty of human connection."

To continue reading, grab book 2 in The Angel Institute Christmas Series.

The angels in training are waiting for you!
Enjoy all the Christmas stories that fill your heart with holiday joy.

Acknowledgments

Writing a book is never a solitary endeavor, and we are profoundly grateful for the incredible team of individuals who have supported us throughout this journey.

First and foremost, we want to express our heartfelt thanks to our amazing beta readers: Rolayne, Marissa, and Renee. Your keen insights, thoughtful feedback, and unwavering enthusiasm have been invaluable. You truly are the best beta readers we could have hoped for, and this series is better because of your contributions.

A special thank you goes to Richard for his meticulous consistency read. Your eagle eye for detail and ability to catch those elusive inconsistencies that somehow slip through have been instrumental in polishing our work to a shine.

We are deeply appreciative of Shaylee for her unwavering support and for helping us launch the Angels Unscripted podcast. Your creativity and dedication have opened up new avenues for us to connect with our readers and share the world of the Angel Institute.

To our wonderful reviewers, we cannot thank you enough. Your thoughtful words and enthusiasm for our books have been a constant source of motivation. Your efforts in spreading the word about the Angel Institute series have been crucial in helping us reach new readers. We are truly grateful for your support and advocacy.

Lastly, to our readers – thank you for embarking on this heavenly adventure with us. Your love for our characters and stories makes all the late nights and rewrites worthwhile.

This series is a labor of love, made possible by the collective efforts of many. We are blessed to have such an incredible community surrounding us, and we thank you all from the bottom of our hearts.

Book Club Questions

Hello, fellow readers!

We're excited you've chosen *Angel Institute: Your Assignment: Ren* for your book club. Now that you've journeyed through Ren's struggles as he learns more about friendship and Christmas, it's time to dive deeper into the heart of the story.

These questions are designed to get you thinking about the bigger picture—the themes, character arcs, and those "aha!" moments that made the story come alive.

Whether you're pondering the challenges faced by our guardian angels in training or dissecting the complexities of human nature, we hope these questions will enrich your reading experience and lead to some enlightening discussions.

So grab your favorite beverage, settle in with your book club, and let's explore the heavenly and earthly realms of Angel Institute together. Happy discussing!

1. How does Arthur's perspective as an angel-in-training add to the story? How might the narrative have been different if told entirely from Ren or Sadie's point of view?

2. Discuss the symbolism of the Christmas season in the book. How does it enhance the themes of love, friendship, and personal growth?

3. How does Ren's fear of repeating his parents' mistakes impact his relationship with Sadie? Can you relate to his hesitation?

4. What role does the town of Benton Falls play in the story? How does the small-town setting contribute to the plot and character development?

5. Analyze the character of Ethan. How does his presence affect Ren and Sadie's relationship? Do you think he was necessary for the story?

6. Discuss the evolution of Ren and Sadie's friendship throughout the book. At what point did you realize their relationship was changing?

7. How does Arthur's own understanding of friendship and love change throughout the story? What lessons does he learn from Ren and Sadie?

8. What do you think about the author's portrayal of Heaven and the angel training process? How does it compare to other depictions you've encountered?

9. Examine the theme of vulnerability in the book. How do different characters struggle with being vulnerable, and how do they overcome it?

10. Discuss the significance of the elementary school playground in Ren and Sadie's story. Why do you think the author chose this location for their reconciliation?

11. How does the author use humor throughout the book? Which moments or lines did you find particularly funny or endearing?

12. What role do secondary characters like Mrs. Henderson play in moving the plot forward?

13. Analyze the Christmas Eve scene in the town square. How does it serve as a climax for both the romantic plot and Arthur's mission?

14. How does the book explore the idea that love and friendship are interconnected? Do you agree with this perspective?

15. Discuss Arthur's initial reluctance to engage with human emotions. How does this change over the course of the story?

16. What do you think about the pacing of Ren and Sadie's relationship? Did their get-together feel rushed or well-timed?

17. How does the book handle the theme of overcoming past traumas and fears in relationships?

18. Discuss the epilogue from Arthur's perspective. How does it tie together the themes of the book?

19. If you could ask the author one question about the book, what would it be?

20. How does this book compare to other holiday romances you've read? What makes it unique or memorable?

Also by Erica Penrod

Billionaire Bachelor Cove Series

Cowboy Reality Romance Series

Heaven and A Cowboy Series

My Heart Channel Romance Series

Country Brides Cowboy Boots Series

Mountain Cove Series

Billionaire Academy Series

The Lone Horse Ranch

Snowed In For Christmas Series

Diamond Cove Romantic Comedy Series

By E.B Penrod

Ever Eden

About the Author

Erica is a romance-loving storyteller, a certified organizer, and Diet Pepsi enthusiast, who has written over 25 contemporary romance novels. Inspired by her family's rodeo lifestyle, her stories often feature galloping horses and wild romance. But that's not all! When she's not penning heart-fluttering tales, Erica transforms into E.B. Penrod, crafting enchanting romantasy novels. Whether you're in the mood for a swoon-worthy love story or something with a supernatural twist, Erica's got you covered.